LEGENDS & STORIES
OF IRELAND

Here's to the best o' good spirits

An ounce of mirth is worth a pound of sorrow—*Chrononhotonthologus*
Qui vit sans folie, n'est pas si sage qu'il le croit—*Rochefoucault*
Legend-i—Legend-o—Legend-um—*Hoole's Terminations*

LEGENDS & STORIES OF IRELAND

Samuel Lover

NONSUCH

First published 1831
Copyright © in this edition 2006
Nonsuch Publishing Ltd

Nonsuch Publishing Limited
The Mill, Brimscombe Port, Stroud, Gloucestershire, GL5 2QG
www.nonsuch-publishing.com

For comments or suggestions, please email the editor of this series at:
classics@tempus-publishing.com

Nonsuch Publishing Ltd is an imprint of Tempus Publishing Group

British Library Cataloguing in Publication Data.
A catalogue record for this book is available from the British Library.

ISBN 1-84588-200-8
ISBN-13 (from January 2007) 978-1-84588-200-6

Typesetting and origination by Nonsuch Publishing Limited
Printed in Great Britain by Oaklands Book Services Limited

CONTENTS

INTRODUCTION TO THE MODERN EDITION

In 1800, THREE YEARS AFTER THE birth of Samuel Lover, the British and Irish parliaments passed the Act of Union which, on 1 January 1801, would lead to the creation of the United Kingdom of Great Britain and Ireland. Since the twelfth century Ireland had been under English and, later, British rule (even if, at times, their writ ran only as far as the Pale, twenty miles from Dublin), and Poyning's Law of 1494 had made the parliament in Dublin effectively subservient to that in London. The Constitution of 1782 had given unprecedented legislative freedom to the Parliament of Ireland, which not all of its members wanted to surrender, but the political situation following the bloody Irish Rebellion of 1798 and the favourable terms proposed by the British meant that the Act was eventually passed with large majorities in both houses.

The Union of Britain and Ireland was, though, only a political union. Ireland retained its cultural identity, which was strengthened by the fact that, unlike the populations of England, Wales and Scotland, the majority of the Irish were (and are) Roman Catholics (most of Ireland's Protestants descended from those 'planted' there by the British in the sixteenth and seventeenth centuries). Also unlike Wales and Scotland, Ireland had a Lord Lieutenant with viceregal powers and a Chief Secretary imposed by the Prime Minister in

London. But, in common with the Scots and the Welsh, although the Irish were ruled by the English, they always remained Irish.

The Society of United Irishmen, who were led by Protestants inspired by the French Revolution, had risen against the British in 1798 and been brutally put down. The subsequent abolition of the Irish parliament led to the emergence of two forms of Irish nationalism: the more radical, violent branch had only a small following in the early nineteenth century, whereas the more moderate, non-violent movement had the support of a larger number of people as well as the Roman Catholic Church. The Catholic Association and the Repeal Association campaigned for Catholic Emancipation (which was achieved in 1829) and the repeal of the Act of Union, rather than the overthrow of British rule through force of arms (which did not come about until 1922). Both were led by Daniel O'Connell, known as 'The Emancipator' and 'The Liberator,' Ireland's foremost politician during the early nineteenth century.

In these circumstances, it is hardly surprising that there was considerable interest in Irish legends and stories: a common heritage unites the people of a country against outsiders. One writer to cater for this taste was William Carleton (1794–1869). His *Traits and Stories of the Irish Peasantry* first appeared in 1830 in two volumes, with a further three volumes being published in 1833 and *Tales of Ireland* in 1834; the five volumes of *Traits and Stories* went through more than fifty editions before his death. Brought up amongst the peasantry of rural Ireland, Carleton was able to describe their lives and their stories with authority and affection.

Samuel Lover, however, came from a very different background. The son of a stockbroker, he was born in Dublin in 1797 and began his career as a painter, being elected to the Royal Hibernian Academy in 1828, at the age of thirty-one. His peculiar talent was for miniature portraits, and he painted a number of the Irish aristocracy; one of his best-known portraits was of Niccolò Paganini, the celebrated virtuoso violinist, painted during his visit to Dublin, which was exhibited at the Royal Academy in London. He was one of the first writers for the *Dublin University Magazine* but it was with *Legends and Stories of Ireland*, published in two parts, in 1831 and 1834, and illustrated by himself, that he made his name as an author.

As well as a painter and a writer, Lover was a musician and, after he moved to London in 1835, he was well received in Society, often appearing at the fashionable receptions of the Countess of Blessington, where he sang a number of his songs. They proved so popular that he published them, as *Songs and Ballads*, in 1839. Lady Blessington's receptions were not only an opportunity for Lover to display his musical prowess, they were also a way for him to meet influential people. Amongst his fellow guests was Charles Dickens, with whom Lover was associated in the founding of *Bentley's Miscellany*, the magazine in which Dickens would serialise *Oliver Twist*. Through moving in the right circles, he was asked to paint the ambassador of the Nawab of Awadh, who was visiting London, and Lord Brougham, the Lord Chancellor, in his official robes.

Irish folklore was a recurrent theme of Lover's ballads, and one of them, 'Rory O'More,' about the principal organiser of the Irish Rebellion of 1641, proved so popular that he later developed it into a novel, *Rory O'More: a National Romance*, which was first published in 1837 and later dramatised for the Adelphi Theatre, the first of several plays to be written by him. *Handy Andy: an Irish Tale* followed in 1842 and *Treasure Trove* in 1884; *The Lyrics of Ireland*, which he edited, appeared in 1858 and *Metrical Tales and Other Poems* in 1860. He returned to Dublin some years before his death, but died in St Helier, on the island of Jersey, where he had gone for his health, in 1860.

PREFACE

T HOUGH THE SOURCES WHENCE THESE stories are derived are open
to every one, yet chance or choice may prevent thousands
from making such sources available; and, though the village crone
and mountain guide have many hearers, still their circle is so
circumscribed that most of what I have ventured to lay before my
reader, is, for the first time, made tangible to the greater portion of
those who do me the favour to become such.

In one story, alone (Paddy the Piper), I have no claim to authorship;
and this I take the earliest opportunity of declaring, although I have
a distinct note to the same effect at the end of the article itself; and,
as I have entered upon my confessions, it is, perhaps, equally fair
to state that, although most of the tales are authentic, there is one
purely my own invention; namely, "The Gridiron."

Many of them were originally intended merely for the diversion
of a few friends round my own fireside; there, recited in the manner
of those from whom I heard them, they first made their *début*, and
the flattering reception they met on so minor a stage, led to their
appearance before larger audiences;—subsequently, I was induced
to publish two of them in the DUBLIN LITERARY GAZETTE, and the
favourable notice from contemporary prints, which they received,
has led to the publication of the present volume.

I should not have troubled the reader with this account of the
"birth, parentage, and education" of my literary bantlings, but to

have it understood that some of them are essentially *oral* in their character, and, I fear, suffer materially when reduced to writing. This I mention *en passant* to the critics; and if I meet but half as good-natured *readers* as I have hitherto found *auditors*, I shall have cause to be thankful. But, previously to the perusal of the following pages, there are a few observations that I feel are necessary, and which I shall make as concise as possible.

Most of the stories are given in the manner of the peasantry; and this has led to some peculiarities that might be objected to, were not the cause explained—namely, frequent digressions in the course of the narrative, occasional adjurations, and certain words unusually spelt. As regards the first, I beg to answer, that the stories would be deficient in national character without it; the Irish are so imaginative, that they never tell a story straightforward, but constantly indulge in episode: for the second, it is only fair to say, that in most cases the Irish peasant's adjurations are not meant to be in the remotest degree irreverent, but arise merely from the impassioned manner of speaking, which an excitable people are prone to; and I trust that such oaths as "thunder-and-turf," or maledictions, as "bad cess to you," will not be considered very offensive. Nay, I will go farther, and say, that their frequent exclamations of "Lord be praised,"— "God betune us and harm," &c., have their origin in a deeply reverential feeling, and a reliance on the protection of Providence. As for the orthographical dilemmas into which an attempt to spell their peculiar pronunciation has led me, I have ample and most successful precedent in Mr Banim's works. Some general observations, however, it may not be irrelevant to introduce here, on the pronunciation of certain sounds in the English language by the Irish peasantry.—And here I wish to be distinctly understood, that I speak only of the midland and western districts of Ireland—and chiefly of the latter.

They are rather prone to curtailing their words; *of,* for instance, is very generally abbreviated into *o'* or *i'*, except when a succeeding vowel demands a consonant; and even in that case they would substitute *v.* The letters *d* and *t,* as finals, they scarcely ever sound; for example, pond, hand, slept, kept, are pronounced *pon, han, slep, kep*. These letters, when followed by a vowel, are sounded as if the aspirate *h* intervened, as tender, letter,—*tindher, letther*. Some sounds they sharpen, and *vice versa*. The letter *e*, for instance, is mostly pronounced like *i* in the word litter, as *lind* for lend, *mind* for mend, &c.; but there are exceptions to this rule—Saint Kevin, for example, which they pronounce K*a*vin. The letter *o* they sound like *a* in some words, as off, *aff* or *av*—thus softening *f* into *v*; beyond, *beyant*— thus sharpening the final *d* to *t,* and making an exception to the custom of not sounding *d* as a final; in others they alter it to *ou*—as old, *owld*. Sometimes *o* is even converted into *i*—as spoil, *spile*. In a strange spirit of contrariety, while they alter the sound of *e* to that of *i,* they substitute the latter for the former sometimes—as hinder, *hendher*—cinder, *cendher. s* they soften into *z*—us, *uz*. There are other peculiarities which this is not an appropriate place to dilate upon. I have noticed the most obvious. Nevertheless, even these are liable to exceptions, as the peasantry are quite governed by ear—as in the word of, which is variously sound *o', i', ov, av*, or *iv*, as best suits their pleasure.

It is unnecessary to remark, how utterly unsystematic I have been in throwing these few remarks together. Indeed, to classify (if it were necessary) that which has its birth in ignorance, would be a very perplexing undertaking. But I wished to notice these striking peculiarities of the peasant pronunciation, which the reader will have frequent occasion to observe in the following pages; and, as a further assistance, I have added a short glossary.

INTRODUCTION

AFTER MY STORIES WERE PRINTED, I began to think what name I should give the volume: and this has puzzled me more than writing it. Though the matter in the following pages is perfectly new, and *unlike any thing which has gone before it*, yet the name that I have been obliged to adopt might lead the public to infer that a certain resemblance cannot but attach where a similarity of title exists, and that a family likeness must follow a family name. This, I beg to say, is not the case; and with the extensive family of "Legends," (fairy or otherwise), "Stories," "Traits," "Sketches," &c., there is not a relationship, even within the seventh degree. So much the worse, perhaps, for its goodness; but I am anxious to plead for its *novelty* only, and therefore has giving it a name been no small trouble to me.

What's in a name?

says Shakspeare; but, did he live in our days, he would know its value. In whatsoever light you view it—in whatsoever scale it may be weighed—name is a most important concern now-a-days. In fashion (*place aux dames*), literature, politics, arts, sciences, &c., &c., name does wonders—it might be almost said every thing—whether for the introduction of a measure in Parliament, or in the length of a waist, for the success of a bad book, a new system, or an old picture.

Name, like the first blow, is half the battle. Impressed with this conviction, every huxter now calls his hovel a PROVISION STORE—a barber's shop is elevated into a *Magasin des Modes*—the long line of teachers, under the names of French-master, dancing-master, fencing-master, music-master, and all the other masters, have dignified themselves with the self-bestowed title of "PROFESSOR"—a snuff and tobacco shop is metamorphosed, for the benefit of all "true believers," into a "cigar *divan;*"—and, in St Stephen's-green, who does not remember the "PANTHEON PHUSITEKNIKON?" which, being rendered into English, by Mr B ——, the ironmonger, proprietor of the same, meant—"Pots, pans, and kettles to mend."

Nay, the very vendors of soaps, cosmetics, and wig-oil, seem to understand the importance of this pass to public patronage, and storm its difficult heights accordingly, with the most jaw-breaking audacity. We have Rowland's *Kalydor*—Turkish *Sidki-Areka*, or Betel-nut Charcoal, Milk of Roses, &c., &c. A circumnavigation of the globe is undertaken to replenish the vocabularies, and the Arctic regions are ransacked for "Bear's Grease," and the Tropics are rifled for *"Macassar Oil."*

Enviable name!—Thou shalt live to future ages, when thy ingenious inventor shall be no more!—when the heads thou hast anointed shall have pressed their last pillow! Nay, when the very humbug that bears thy name shall have fallen into disuse—thou, felicitous name! shalt be found embalmed in "immortal verse," for the mighty Byron has enshrined thee in his couplets:—

> In virtues nothing earthly could surpass her,
> Save thine 'incomparable oil,' Macassar.

So saith Byron of Donna Inez.

Descending still lower than the venders as aforesaid noticed, the *very dogs* are concerned in this all-important thing, a name; for you know the memorable old saying, that declares, "You may as well kill a dog as give him a bad name."

Pardon, then, the anxiety of an unfortunate dog like me, for some name that may lift him out of his own insignificance: or, to pursue the image, may "help a lame dog over the stile."—But a name that I could wish for my book is not to be had; so many authors have been before me, that all the good names are gone, like the good hats at a party. It must only put the best that is left on the head of my poor little book, and send it into the world to take its chance, but lest any prejudice should arise against it, from wearing a CAUBEEN instead of a beaver, I had better tell my readers what they shall find in the following pages. And as, in the Island of Laputa, there were certain functionaries called "flappers," whose duty it was to keep people alive to their business, by hitting them in the face with bladders charged with air and a few peas, I am now going to undertake the office of flapper, to awaken people to a notion of what they are to expect in the *terra incognita* before them—though I shall not indulge in so *inflated* a manner of doing so as the Laputans.

But time is a treasure (though one would not suppose I think so, from the way in which I am now wasting it) and as its return is beyond our power, we should not take that from others which we cannot restore. Don't be afraid, sweet reader—I am not going to moralise; it is what I am seldom guilty of: besides, you might, haply, think of Monsieur Jaques, when you hear

> The *fool* thus moralise upon the time;

and I have no desire that "your lungs begin to crow like Chanticleer" at *me*, however I hope they may at *my stories*.

But to the point: I do not wish, I say, to swindle respectable gentlemen or ladies out of their time; therefore, I beg to recommend all serious persons—your masters of arts, your explorers of science, star-gazing philosophers, and moon-struck maidens, LL.D.s, F.R.S.s, and all other *three-letter* gentlemen, to lay down this book, even at this very *period*.—if you be of the same mind with that facetious gentleman, Rigdum Funnidos, and agree with him, that

An ounce of mirth is worth a pound of sorrow,

then, I say, you may as well go on, and throw away your time in laughing at my book, as in any other way whatsoever.

Deep in the western wilds of Ireland have I been gathering these native productions, called *Rigmaroles*, to contribute to your pleasure. If you be a lover of rhodomontade, or, as Paddy calls it, *Rogermontade*, you had better, in true Irish fashion, "take a short stick to your hand," and trudge away boldly through my post octavo. As for ladies who are

> Darkly, deeply, beautifully blue,
> As some one somewhere sings about the sea,
> (Excuse me, Byron, that I steal from you)—
> Do not, like Nanny—do not gang with me!

for there are no raptures nor Italian quotations for you. But if you have not outlived the charm which the wonders of the nursery tale produced, or if you are yet willing to commit such a vulgarism as a laugh, pray take my arm, and allow me to lead you into the next page.

I would say a great deal more, but that I fear, instead of fulfilling my office of "flapper," I should only set people to sleep. I shall therefore conclude, by saying a word or two about the illustrations.

They are my first attempt upon copper; and whatever affinity there maybe between that and brass, which, thanks to my country, I may not be so much unused to, yet I can assure the critics there is a marvellous difference between etching and impudence. Let me not be accused then of the latter, in having attempted the former, but some indulgence be granted to a *coup d'essai*. So much for the *executive* part; and, for the *designs,* I beg to say a few words more, which I shall offer in the form of a

Notice
TO
The Antiquarian Society.

Should any such august personage as an Antiquary chance to cast his eyes over the illustrations of this little book, it is humbly requested that his repose be not disturbed in fancied anachronisms in the costumes. We say, *fancied*—for considerable pains have been bestowed in ascertaining the true style of dress in which each of our heroes flourished, from the narrators of their several histories—and who could possibly know so well?

Upon the testimony of the aforesaid credible authority, King O'Toole wore a snuff-coloured-square-cut coat, with hanging sleeves, and silver buttons—black velvet inexpressibles, trunk hose, and high-heeled shoes, with buckles.

This monarch is said to have had a *foible* (what monarch is without?) in paying particular attention to his *queue,* of which he was not a little vain. He constantly, moreover, wore a crown upon his head, which Joe Irwin protested was "full half a hundredweight o' goold." Had this fact been known to the commentators upon Shakspeare, they might have been better able to appreciate that line of the immortal bard's—

Uneasy lies the head that wears a crown!

Saint Kevin had a little failing of his own also—an inconsiderate indulgence in smoking, which, all antiquaries are aware, is an ancient usage in Ireland. The pipe in his hat, therefore, is especially indicative of the Saint. It is further understood (such pains have been taken to be accurate) that the Saint "blew his cloud" from the corner of his mouth, and not directly forwards, as commonly practised. In what slight things is *character* developed!—It is quite natural that a circumventing person, like Saint Kevin, should have dealt in the *puff oblique.*

GLOSSARY

ALPEEN—A cudgel.

BAD SCRAM—Bad food.

BAD WIN' }
BAD CESS } Malediction. Cess is an abbreviation of success

BAITHERSHIN'—It may be so.

BALLYRAG—To scold.

CAUBEEN—An old hat. Strictly, a *little* old hat. *Een*, in Irish, is diminutive.

COLLEEN DHAS—Pretty girl.

COMETHER—Corruption of hither. "Putting his comether" means forcing his acquaintance.

GOMMOCH—A simpleton.

HARD WORD—Hint.

HUNKERS—Haunches.

KIMMEENS—Sly tricks.

MACHREE—My dear.

MAVOURNEEN—My darling.

MUSHA!—An exclamation, as "Oh, my!" "Oh, la!"

NOGGIN—A small wooden drinking vessel.

PHILLELEW—An outcry.

SPALPEEN—A contemptible person.

STRAVAIG—To ramble.

ULICAN—The funeral cry.

WAKE—Watching the body of the departed previously
    to interment.
WEIRASTHRU!—Mary have pity!

1.   This I have spelled as it is pronounced. The correct spelling of the
     phrase would be a very puzzling concern indeed—as, in the original, it
     is equally complex in construction to the French *qu'est ce que c'est que
     cela*. I have pursued the same rule with all the other Irish expressions
     in the Glossary:—First, because the true spellings are very unlike
     the sounds—*Weira*, for instance, is written in Irish, *Mhuira;* and next,
     because my object is only to give the reader an explanatory reference to
     the "Stories," not to write an Irish vocabulary—which, indeed, I am not
     prepared to do.

King O'Toole and St Kevin

A Legend of Glendalough

By that lake, whose gloomy shore
Sky-lark never warbles o'er,
Where the cliff pangs high and steep,
Young Saint Kevin stole to sleep.

Moore

W HO HAS NOT READ OF St Kevin, celebrated as he has been by
Moore in the melodies of his native land, with whose wild
and impassioned music he has so intimately entwined his name?
Through him, in the beautiful ballad whence the epigraph of this
story is quoted, the world already knows that the sky lark, through
the intervention of the saint, never startles the morning with its joy
note in the lonely valley of Glendalough. In the same ballad the
unhappy passion which the saint inspired, and the "unholy blue" eyes
of Kathleen, and the melancholy fate of the heroine by the saint's
being "unused to the melting mood," are also celebrated; as well as

the superstitious *finale* of the legend, in the spectral appearance of
the love-lorn maiden:

> And her ghost was seen to glide
> Gently o'er the fatal tide.

Thus has Moore given, within the limits of a ballad, the spirit
of two legends of Glendalough, which otherwise the reader might
have been put to the trouble of reaching after a more round-about
fashion. But luckily for those coming after him, one legend he has
left to be

—touched by a hand more unworthy—

and instead of a lyrical essence, the raw material in prose is offered,
nearly *verbatim* as it was furnished to me by that celebrated guide
and *bore*, Joe Irwin, who traces his descent in a direct line from the
old Irish kings, and warns the public in general that "there's a power
of them spalpeens sthravaigin' about, sthrivin' to put their *comether*
upon the quol'ty, (quality,') and callin' themselves Irwin (knowin',
the thieves o' the world, how his name had gone far and near, as the
rale guide), for to deceave dacent people; but never for to b'lieve
the likes—for it was only mulvatherin people they wor." For my
part I promised never to put faith in any but himself; and the old
rogue's self-love being satisfied, we set out to explore the wonders
of Glendalough. On arriving at a small ruin, situated on the south
eastern side of the lake, my guide assumed an air of importance, and
led me into the ivy-covered remains, through a small square whose
simple structure gave evidence of it early date: a lintel of stone lay
across two upright supporters after the fashion of such remains in
Ireland.

"This, Sir," said my guide, putting himself in an attitude, "is the
chapel of King O'Toole —av coorse y'iv often heerd o' Kin O'Toole,
your honor?"

"Never," said I,

"Musha, thin, do you tell me so?" said he; "by Gor, I thought all the world, far and near, heerd o' King O'Toole—well! well!! but the darkness of mankind is ontellible. Well, Sir, you must know as you didn't hear it before that there was wanst a king, called King O'Toole, who was a fine ould king in the ould ancient times, long ago; and it was him that ownded the Churches in the airly days."

"Surely," said I, "the Churches were not in King O'Toole's time?"

"Oh, by no manes, your honour—throth, it's yourself that's right enough there; but you know the place is called 'The Churches,' bekase they wor built *afther* by St Kavin, and wint by the name o' the Churches iver more; and therefore, av coorse, the place bein' so called, I say that the king ownded the Churches—and why not, Sir, seein' 'twas his birthright, time out o' mind, beyant the flood? Well, the king, you see, was the right sort—he was the *rale* boy, and loved sport as he loved his life, and huntin' in partic'lar; and from the risin' o' the sun, up he got, and away he wint over the mountains beyant afther the deer: and the fine times them wor; for the deer was as plinty thin, aye throth, far plintyer than the sheep is now; and that's the way it was with the king, from the crow o' the cock to the song o' the redbreast.

"In this counthry, Sir," added he, speaking parenthetically in an undertone, "we think it onlooky to kill the redbreast, for the robin is God's own bird."

Then, elevating his voice to its former pitch, he proceeded:— "Well, it was all mighty good, as long as the king had his health; but, you see, in coorse o' time, the king grewn owld, by raison he was stiff in his limbs, and when he got sthriken in years, his heart failed him, and he was lost intirely for want o' divarshin, bekase he couldn't go a huntin' no longer; and, by dad, the poor king was obleeged at last for to get a goose to divart him."

Here an involuntary smile was produced by this regal mode of recreation of "the royal game of goose."

"Oh, you may laugh if you like," said he, half affronted, "but it's thruth I'm tellin' you; and the way the goose divarted him was this-a–way: you see, the goose used for to swim acrass the lake, and go down divin' for throut, (and not finer throut in all Ireland, than the same throut,) and cotch fish on a Friday for the king, and flew every other day round about the lake divartin' the poor king, that you'd think he'd break his sides laughin' at the frolicksome tricks av his goose; so in coorse o' time the goose was the greatest pet in the counthry, and the biggest rogue, and diverted the king to no end, and the poor king was as happy as the day was long. So that's the way it was; and all went on mighty well, antil, by dad, the goose got sthricken in years, as well as the king, and grewn stiff in the limbs, like her masther, and couldn't divart him no longer; and then it was that the poor king was lost complate, and didn't know what in the wide world to do, seein' he was done out of all divarshin, by raison that the goose was no more in the flower of her blame.

"Well, the king was nigh hand broken-hearted, and melancholy intirely, and was walkin' one mornin' by the edge of the lake lamentin' his cruel fate, an' thinkin' o' drownin' himself that could get no divarshin in life, when all of a suddint, turnin' round the corner beyant; who should he meet but a mighty dacent young man comin' up to him.

"'God save you,' says the king (for the king was a civil-spoken gintleman, by all accounts,) 'God save you,' says he to the young man.

"'God save you kindly,' says the young man to him back again; 'God save you,' says he, 'King O'Toole.'

"'Thrue for you,' says the king, 'I am King O'Toole,' says he, 'prince and Plennypennytinchery o' these parts,' says he; 'but how kem ye to know that?' says he.

"'O, never mind,' says Saint Kavin.

"For you see," said old Joe, in his undertone again, and looking very knowingly, "it *was* Saint Kavin, sure enough—the saint himself in disguise, and nobody else. 'Oh, never mind,' says he, 'I know more than that,' says he, 'nor twice that.'

"'And who are you?' said the king, 'that makes so bowld—who are you, at all at all?'

"'Oh, never you mind,' says Saint Kavin, 'who I am; you'll know more o' me before we part, King O'Toole,' says he.

"'I'll be proud o' the knowledge o' your acquaintance, sir,' says the king, mighty p'lite.

"'Troth, you may say that,' says St Kavin. 'And now, may I make bowld to ax, how is your goose, King O'Toole?' says he.

"'Blur-an-agers, how kem you to know about my goose?' says the king.

"'O, no matther; I was given to undherstand it,' says Saint Kavin.

"'Oh, that's a folly to talk,' says the king; 'bekase myself and my goose is private frinds,' says he, 'and no one could tell you,' says he, 'barrin' the fairies.'

"'Oh thin, it wasn't the fairies,' says Saint Kavin; 'for I'd have you to know,' says he, 'that I don't keep the likes o' sitch company.'

"'You might do worse then, my gay fellow,' says the king; 'for it's *they* could show you a crock o' money as aisy as kiss hand; and that's not to be sneezed at,' says the king, 'by a poor man,' says he.

"'Maybe I've a betther way of making money myself,' says the saint.

"'By gor,' says the king, 'barrin' you're a coiner,' says he, 'that's impossible!'

"'I'd scorn to be the like, my lord!' says Saint Kavin, mighty high, 'I'd scorn to be the like,' says he.

"'Then, what are you?' says the king, 'that makes money so aisy, by your own account.'

"'I'm an honest man,' says Saint Kavin.

"'Well, honest man,' says the king, 'and how is it you make your money so aisy?'

"'By makin' ould look as good as new,' says Saint Kavin.

"'Blur-an-ouns, is it a tinker you are?' says the king.

"'No,' says the saint; 'I'm no tinker by thrade, King O'Toole; I've a betther thrade than a tinker,' says he—'what would you say,' says he, 'if I made your old goose as good as new.'

"My dear, at the word o' makin' his goose as good as new, you'd think the poor ould king's eyes was ready to jump out iv his head, 'and,' says he—'troth thin I'd give you more money nor you could count,' says he, 'if you did the like and I'd be behoulden to you into the bargain.'

"'I scorn your dirty money,' says Saint Kavin.

"'Faith then, I'm thinkin' a thrifle o' change would do you no harm,' says the king, lookin' up sly at the old *caubeen* that Saint Kavin had on him.

"'I have a vow agin it,' says the saint; 'and I am book sworn,' says he, 'never to have goold, silver, or brass in my company.'

"'Barrin' the thrifle you can't help,' says the king, mighty 'cute, and looking him straight in the face.

"'You just hot it,' says Saint Kavin; 'but though I can't take money,' says he, 'I could take a few acres o' land, if you'd give them to me.'

"'With all the veins o' my heart,' says the king, 'if you can do what you say.'

"'Thry me!' says Saint Kavin. 'Call down your goose here,' says he, 'and I'll see what I can do for her.'

"'With that, the king whistled, and down kem the poor goose, all as one as a hound, waddlin' up to the poor ould cripple, her masther, and as like him as two *pays*. The minute the saint clapt his eyes an the goose, 'I'll do the job for you,' says he, 'King O'Toole!'

"'By *Jaminee,*' says King O'Toole, 'if you do, bud I'll say you're the cleverest fellow in the sivin parishes.'

"'Oh, by dad,' says Saint Kavin, 'you must say more nor that—my horn's not so soft all out,' says he, 'as to repair your ould goose for nothin'; what'll you gi' me, if I do the job for you?—that's the chat,' says Saint Kavin.

"'I'll give you whatever you ax,' says the king; 'isn't that fair?'

"'Divil a fairer,' says the saint; 'that's the way to do business. Now,' says he, 'this is the bargain I'll make with you, King O'Toole: will you gi' me all the ground the goose flies over, the first offer afther I make her as good as new?'

"'I will,' says the king.

"'You won't go back o' your word?' says Saint Kavin.

"'Honour bright!' says King O'Toole, howldin' out his fist."

Here old Joe, after applying his hand to his mouth, and making a sharp, blowing sound (something like "*thp*,") extended it to illustrate the action.[2]

"'Honour bright,' says Saint Kavin, back agin, 'it's a bargain,' says he. 'Come here!' says he to the poor ould goose—'come here you unfort'nate ould cripple,' says he, 'and it's *I* that 'ill make you the sportin' bird.'

"With that, my dear, he tuk up the goose by the two wings—'criss o' my crass an you,' says he, markin' her to grace with the blessed sign at the same minute—and throwin' her up in the air, 'whew!' says he, jist givin' her a blast to help her; and with that, my jewel, she tuk to her heels, flyin' like one o' the aigles themselves, and cuttin' as many capers as a swallow before a shower of rain. Away she wint down there, right fornist you, along the side o' the clift, and flew over Saint Kavin's bed (that is where Saint Kavin's bed is *now,* but was not *thin,* by raison it wasn't made, but was conthrived afther by Saint Kavin himself, that the women might lave him alone), and on with her undher Lugduff, and round the ind av the lake there, far beyant where you see the watherfall (though indeed it's no watherfall at all now, but only a poor dhribble iv a thing; but if you seen it in the winther, it id do your heart good, and it roarin' like mad, and as white as the dhriven snow, and rowlin' down the big rocks before it, all as one as childher playin' marbles)—and on with her thin right over the lead mines o' Luganure (that is where the lead mines is *now*, but was not *thin*, by raison they worn't discovered, *but was all goold in Saint Kavin's time*). Well, over the ind o' Luganure she flew, stout and sturdy, and round the other ind av the *little* lake, by the Churches, (that is, *av coorse*, where the Churches is *now*, but was not *thin*, by raison they wor not built, but afterwards by St Kavin), and over the big hill here over your head, where you see the big clift—(and that clift in the mountain was made by Fan Ma Cool, where he cut it acrass with a big swoord, that he got made a purpose by a blacksmith out o' Rathdrum, a cousin av his own, for to fight a joyant [giant] that darr'd him an the Curragh o' Kildare; and he thried the swoord first an the mountain, and cut it down into a gap, as is plain to this day; and faith sure enough, it's the same sauce he sarv'd the joyant, soon and suddent, and chopped him in two like a pratie, for the glory of his sowl and owld Ireland)—well, down she flew over the clift, and flutterin' over the wood there at Poulanass (where I showed you the purty watherfall—and by the same token, last Thursday was a twelve-month sence, a young lady, Miss Rafferty by name, fell into the same watherfall, and was nigh hand drownded—and indeed would be to this day, but for a young man that jumped in afther her; indeed a smart slip iv a young man he was—he was out o' Francis-street, I hear, and coorted her sence, and they wor married, I'm given to undherstand—and indeed a purty couple they wor). Well—as I said—afther flutterin' over the wood a little bit, to *plaze* herself, the goose flew down, and lit at the fut o' the king, as fresh as a daisy, afther flyin' roun' his dominions, just as if she hadn't flew the perch.

"Well, my dear, it was a beautiful sight to see the king standin' with his mouth open, lookin' at his poor ould goose flyin' as light as a lark, and betther nor ever she was: and when she lit at his fut, he patted her an the head, and '*ma vourneen*,' says he, 'but you are the *darlint* o' the world.'

"'And what do you say to me,' says Saint Kavin, 'for makin' her the like?'

"'By gor,' says the king, 'I say nothin' bates the art o' man, barrin'[3] the bees.'

"'And do you say no more nor that?' says Saint Kavin.

"'And that I'm beholden to you,' says the king.

"'But will you gi'e me all the ground the goose flewn over?' says Saint Kavin

"'I will,' says King O'Toole, 'and you're welkim to it,' says he, 'though it's the last acre I have to give.'

"'But you'll keep your word thrue?' says the saint.

"'As thrue as the sun,' says the king.

"'It's well for you,' (says Saint Kavin, mighty sharp)—'it's well for you, King O'Toole, that you said that word,' says he; 'for if you didn't say that word, *the divil receave the bit o' your goose id ever fly agin*,' says Saint Kavin.

"Oh, you needn't laugh," said old Joe, half offended at detecting the trace of a suppressed smile; "you needn't laugh, *for it's thruth I'm tellin' you*.

"Well, whin the king was as good as his word, Saint Kavin was plazed with him, and thin it was that he made himself known to the king. 'And,' says he, 'King O'Toole, you're a dacent man,' says he; 'for I only kem here to *thry you*. You don't know me,' says he, 'bekase I'm disguised.'"[4]

"'Troth, then, you 're right enough,' says the king, 'I didn't perceave it,' says he; 'for indeed I never seen the sign o' sper'ts an you.'

"'Oh! that's not what I mane,' says Saint Kavin; 'I mane I'm deceavin' you all out, and that I'm not myself at all.'

"'Blur-an-agers! thin,' says the king, 'if you're not yourself, who are you?'

"'I'm Saint Kavin,' said the saint, blessin' himself.

"'Oh, queen iv heaven!' says the king, makin' the sign o' the crass betune his eyes, and fallin' down on his knees before the saint. 'Is it the great Saint Kavin,' says he, 'that I've been discoorsin' all this time without knowin' it,' says he, 'all as one as if he was a lump iv a *gossoon*?—and so you're a saint?' says the king.

"'I am,' says Saint Kavin.

"'By gor, I thought I was only talking to a dacent boy[5],' says the king.

"'Well, you know the differ now,' says the saint. 'I'm Saint Kavin,' says he, 'the greatest of all the saints.'

"For Saint Kavin, you must know, Sir," added Joe, treating me to another parenthesis, "Saint Kavin is counted the greatest of all the saints, bekase he went to school with the prophet Jeremiah.

"Well, my dear, that's the way that the place kem, all at wanst, into the hands of Saint Kavin; for the goose flewn round every individyal acre o' King O'Toole's property you see, *bein' let into the saycret* by Saint Kavin, who was mighty 'cute;[6] and so, when he done the ould king out iv his property for the glory of God, he was *plazed* with him, and he and the king was the best o' frinds iver more afther (for the poor ould king was *doatin'*, you see), and the king had his goose as good as new, to divart him as long as he lived and the saint supported him afther he kem into his property, as I tould you, antil the day iv his death—and that was soon afther; for the poor goose thought he was ketehin' a throut one Friday; but, my jewel, it was a mistake he made—and instead of a throut, it was a thievin' horse-eel;[7] and by gor, instead iv the goose killin' a throut for the king's supper—by dad, the eel killed the king's goose—and small blame to him; but he didn't ate her, bekase be darn't ate what Saint Kavin laid his blessed hands on.

"Howsuindever, the king never recovered the loss iv his goose, though he had her stuffed, (I don't mane stuffed with pratees and inyans, but as a curosity), and presarved in a glass-case for his own divarshin; and the poor king died on the next Michaelmas-day, which was remarkable. *Throth, it's thruth, I'm tellin' you*;—and when he was gone, Saint Kavin gev him an illigant wake and a beautiful berrin'; and more betoken, he *said mass for his sowl, and tuk care av his goose.*"

1.   The Irish peasantry very generally call the higher orders "quality."
2.   This royal mode of concluding a bargain has descended in its original purity from the days of King O'Toole to the present time, and is constantly practised by the Irish peasantry. We believe something of *luck* is attributed to this same sharp blowing we have noticed, and which, for the sake of "ears polite," we have not ventured to call by its right name for, to speak truly, a slight escapement of saliva takes place at the time. It is thus *hansel* is given and received; and many are the virtues attributed by the lower order of the Irish to "fasting spittle."
3.   Barring is constantly used by the Irish peasantry for except.
4.   A person in a state of drunkenness is said to be disguised.
5.   The English reader must not imagine the saint to have been very juvenile, from this expression of the king's. In Ireland, a man in the prime of life is called a "stout *boy.*"
6.   Cunning—an abbreviation of acute.

7. Eels of uncommon size are said to exist in the upper lake of Glendalough:
    the guides invariably tell marvellous stories of them: they describe them
    of forbidding aspect, with manes as large as a horse's. One of these
    "slippery rogues" is said to have amused himself by entering a pasture
    on the borders of the lake, and eating a *cow*—maybe 'twas a *bull*.

LOUGH CORRIB

—These things to hear
Would Desdemona seriously incline.

OTHELLO

I T CHANCED, AMONGST SOME OF the pleasantest adventures of a tour
through the West of Ireland, in 1825, that the house of Mr —— of
—— received me as a guest. The owner of the mansion upheld the
proverbial reputation of his country's hospitality, and his lady was of
singularly winning manners and possessed of much intelligence—an
intelligence, arising not merely from the cultivation resulting from
careful education, but originating also from the attention which
persons of good sense bestow upon the circumstances which come
within the range of their observation.

Thus, Mrs ——, an accomplished Englishwoman, instead
of sneering at the deficiencies which a poorer country than her
own laboured under, was willing to be amused by observing the
difference which exists in the national character of the two people,
in noticing the prevalence of certain customs, superstitions, &c., &c.;
while the popular tales of the neighbourhood had for her a charm,
which enlivened a sojourn in a remote district, that must otherwise
have proved lonely.

To this pleasure was added that of admiration of the natural
beauties with which she was surrounded; the noble chain of the

Mayo mountains, linking with the majestic range of those of Joyce's country, formed no inconsiderable source of picturesque beauty and savage grandeur; and when careering over the waters of Lough Corrib that foamed at their feet, she never sighed for the grassy slopes of Hyde-park, nor that unruffled pond, the Serpentine river.

In the same boat which often bore so fair a charge, have I explored the noble Lough Corrib to its remotest extremity, sailing over the depths of its dark waters, amidst solitudes whose echoes are seldom awakened but by the scream of the eagle.

From this lady I heard some characteristic stories and prevalent superstitions of the country. Many of these she had obtained from an old boatman, one of the crew that manned Mr ——'s boat; and often, as he sat at the helm, he delivered his "round, unvarnished tale;" and, by the way, in no very measured terms either, whenever his subject happened to touch upon the what his country had sustained in her early wars against England, although his liege lady was a native of the hostile land. Nevertheless, the old Corribean (the name somehow has a charmingly savage sound about it) was nothing loth to have his fling at "the invaders"—a term of reproach he always cast upon the English.

Thus skilled in legendary lore, Mrs —— proved an admirable guide to the "lions" of the neighbourhood; and it was previously to a projected visit to the Cave of Cong, that she entered upon some anecdotes relating to the romantic spot, which led her to tell me, that one legend had so particularly excited the fancy of a young lady, a friend of hers, that she wrought it into the form of a little tale, which, she added, had not been considered ill done. "But," said she, "'tis true we were all friends who passed judgment, and only drawing-room critics. You shall therefore judge for yourself, and hearing it before you see the cave, will at least rather increase your interest in the visit." And, forthwith, drawing from a little cabinet a manuscript, she read to me the following tale—much increased in its effect by the sweet voice in which it was delivered.

Manuscript
from the Cabinet of Mrs ——

A Legend of Lough Mask

All things that we ordained festival
Turn from their office to black funeral;
Our instruments, to melancholy bells;
Our wedding cheer, to a sad burial feast;
Our solemn hymns to sullen dirges change;
Our bridal flowers serve for a buried corse,
And all things change them to the contrary.

Romeo and Juliet

The evening was closing fast, as the young Cormac O'Flaherty had reached the highest acclivity of one of the rugged passes of the steep mountains of Joyce's country. He made a brief pause—not to take breath, fair reader—for Cormac needed no breathing time, and would have considered it little short of an insult to have had such a motive attributed to the momentary stand he made, and none that knew the action of the human figure would have thought it; for the

firm footing which one beautifully-formed leg held with youthful firmness on the mountain path, while the other, slightly thrown behind, rested on the half-bent foot, did not imply repose, but rather suspended action. In sooth, young Cormac, to the eye of the painter, might have seemed a living *Antinous*—all the grace of that beautiful antique, all the youth, all the expression of suspended motion were there, with more of vigour and impatience. He paused—not to take breath, Sir Walter Scott; for, like your own Malcolm Graeme,

> Right up Ben Lomond could he press,
> And not a sob his toil confess;

and our young O'Flaherty was not to be outdone in breasting up a mountain side, by the boldest Graeme of them all.

But he lingered for a moment to look back upon a scene at once sublime and gorgeous; and cold must the mortal have been who could have beheld, and had not paused.

On one side, the Atlantic lay beneath him brightly reflecting the glories of an autumnal setting sun, and expanding into a horizon of dazzling light; on the other lay the untrodden wilds before him, stretching amidst the depths of mountain valleys, whence the sunbeam had long since departed, and mists were already wreathing round the overhanging heights, and veiling the distance in vapoury indistinctness: as though you looked into some wizard's glass, and saw the uncertain conjuration of his wand. On the one side all was glory, light, and life—on the other all was awful, still, and almost dark. It was one of Nature's sublimest moments;—such as are seldom witnessed, and never forgotten.[1]

Ere he descended the opposite declivity, Cormac once more bent back his gaze—and now it was not one exclusively of admiration; there was a mixture of scrutiny in his look, and turning to Diarmid, a faithful adherent of his family, and only present companion, he said, "That sunset forebodes a coming storm; does it not, Diarmid?"

"Ay, truly does it," responded the attendant, "and there's no truth in the clouds, if we haven't it soon upon us."

"Then let us speed," said Cormac—"for the high hill and the narrow path must be traversed ere our journey be accomplished." And he sprang down the steep and shingly pass before him, followed by the faithful Diarmid,

> 'Tis sweet to know there is an eye to mark
> Our coming—and grow brighter when we come.

And there *was* a bright eye watching for Cormac, and many a love-taught look did Eva cast over the waters of Lough Mask, impatient for the arrival of the O'Flaherty. "Surely he will be here this evening," thought Eva, "yet the sun is already low, as no distant oars disturb the lovely quiet of the lake—but may he not have tarried beyond the mountains? he has friends there," recollected Eva. But soon the maiden's jealous fancy whispered "he has friends *here* too"—and she reproached him for his delay;—but it was only for a moment.

"The accusing spirit blushed"—as Eva continued her train of conjecture. "'Tis hard to part from pressing friends," thought she, "and Cormac is ever welcome in the hall, and heavily closes the portal after his departing footsteps."

Another glance across the lake. yet unrippled by an oar. The faint outline of the dark grey mountains, whose large masses lie unbroken by the detail which daylight discovers—hazy distance of the lake, whose extremity is undistinguishable from the overhanging cliffs which embrace it—the fading of the western sky—the last lonely rook winging his weary way to the adjacent wood—the flickering flight of the bat across her windows—all—all told Eva that the night was fast approaching; yet Cormac was not come. She turned from the casement with a sigh.—Oh! only those who love can tell how anxious are the moments we pass in watching the approach of the beloved one.

She took her harp: every heroine, to be sure, has a harp: but this was not the pedal harp, that instrument *par excellence* of heroines, but the simple harp of her country, whose single row of brazen wires had often rung to many a sprightly planxty, long, long before the double action of Erard had vibrated to some fantasia from Rossini or Mayerbeer, under the brilliant finger of a Bochsa or a Labarre.

But now the harp of Eva did not ring forth the spirit-stirring planxty, but yielded to her gentlest touch one of the most soothing and plaintive of her native melodies; and to her womanly sensibility, which long expectation had excited, it seemed to breathe an unusual flow of tenderness and pathos, which her heated imagination conjured almost into prophetic wailing. Eva paused—she was alone; the night had closed—her chamber was dark and silent. She burst into tears, and when her spirits became somewhat calmed by this gush of feeling, she arose, and dashing the lingering ear from the long lashes of the most beautiful blue eyes in the world, she hastened to the hall, and sought in the society of others to dissipate those feelings by which she had been overcome.

The night closed over the path of Cormac, and the storm he anticipated had swept across the waves of the Atlantic, and now burst in all its fury over the mountains of Joyce's country. The wind rushed along in wild gusts, bearing in its sweeping eddy heavy dashes of rain, which soon increased to a continuous deluge of enormous drops, rendering the mountain gullies the channel of temporary rivers, and the path that wound along the verge of each precipice so slippery, as to render its passage death to the timid or unwary, and dangerous even to the firmest or most practised foot. But our hero and his attendant strode on—the torrent was resolutely passed, its wild roar audible above the loud thunder-peals that rolled through the startled echoes of the mountains; the dizzy path was firmly trod, its dangers rendered more perceptible by the blue lightnings, half revealing the depths of the abyss beneath; and Cormac and Diarmid still pressed on towards the shores of Lough Mask, unconscious of the interruption that yet awaited them, fiercer than the torrent, and more deadly than the lightning.

As they passed round the base of a projecting crag, that flung its angular masses athwart the ravine through which they wound, a voice of brutal coarseness suddenly arrested their progress with the fiercely uttered word of "Stand!"

Cormac instantly stopped—as instantly his weapon was in his hand; and with searching eye he sought to discover through the gloom, what bold intruder dared cross the path of the O'Flaherty. His tongue now demanded what his eye failed him to make known; and the same rude voice that first addressed him answered, "Thy mortal foe!—thou seek'st thy bride, fond boy, but never shalt thou behold her—never shalt thou share the bed of Eva."

"Thou liest! foul traitor!" cried Cormac fiercely; "avoid my path—avoid it, I say, for death is in it!"

"Thou say'st truly," answered the unknown, with a laugh of horrid meaning; "come on, and thy words shall be made good!"

At this moment a flash of lightning illumined the whole glen with momentary splendour, and discovered to Cormac, a few paces before him, two armed men of gigantic stature, in one of whom he recognised Emman O'Flaherty, one of the many branches of that ancient and extensive family, equally distinguished for his personal prowess and savage temper.

"Ha!" exclaimed Cormac, "is it Emman Dubh?" for the black hair of Emman had obtained for him this denomination of *Black Edward*, a name fearfully suitable to him who bore it.

"Yes," answered he tauntingly, "it is Emman Dubh who waits the coming of his *fair* cousin;—you have said death is in your path— come on, and meet it."

Nothing daunted, however shocked at discovering the midnight waylayer of his path in his own relative, Cormac answered, "Emman Dubh, I have never wronged you; but since you thirst for my blood, and cross my path, on your own head be the penalty.—Stand by me, Diarmid!" said the brave youth; and rushing on his Herculean enemy, they closed in mortal combat.

Had the numbers been equal, the colossal strength of Emman might have found its overmatch in the activity of Cormac, and his skill in the use of his weapon. But oh! the foul, the treacherous Emman—he dared his high-spirited rival to advance, but to entrap him into an ambuscade; for as he rushed upon his foe, past the beetling rock that hung over his path, a third assassin, unseen by the gallant Cormac, lay in wait; and when the noble youth was engaged in the fierce encounter, a blow, dealt him in the back, laid the betrothed of Eva lifeless at the feet of the savage and exulting Emman.

Restlessly had Eva passed that turbulent night—each gust of the tempest, each flash of living flame and burst of thunder awakened her terrors, lest Cormac, the beloved of her soul, were exposed to its fury; but in the lapses of the storm, hope ventured to whisper he yet lingered in the castle of some friend beyond the mountains. The morning dawned, and silently bore witness to the commotion of the elements of the past night. The riven branch of the naked tree, that in one night had been shorn of its leafy beauty; the earth strown with foliage half green, half yellow, ere yet the autumnal alchemy had converted its summer verdure quite to gold, gave evidence that an unusually early storm had been a forerunner of the equinox. The general aspect of nature too, though calm, was cold; the mountains wore a dress of sombre grey, and the small scattered clouds were straggling over the face of heaven, as though they had been rudely riven asunder, and the short and quick lash of the waters upon the shore of Lough Mask, might have told to an accustomed eye, that a longer wave and a whiter foam had broken on its strand a few hours before.

But what is that upthrown upon the beach? And who are those who surround it in such consternation? It is the little skiff that was moored at the opposite side of the lake on the preceding eve, and

was to have borne Cormac to his betrothed bride? And they who
identify the shattered boat are those to whom Eva's happiness is dear;
for it is her father and his attendants, who are drawing ill omens
from the tiny wreck. But they conceal the fact, and the expecting
girl is not told of the evil-boding discovery. But days have come and
gone, and Cormac yet tarries. At length 'tis past a doubt; and the
father of Eva knows his child is widowed ere her bridal— widowed
in heart, a least. And who shall tell the fatal tale to Eva? Who shall
cast the shadow o'er her soul, and make the future darkness? —Alas!
ye feeling souls that ask it, that pause ere you can speak the word that
lights for ever, pause no longer, for Eva knows it. Yes; from tongue to
tongue—by word on word from many a quivering lip, and meanings
darkly given, the dreadful certainty at last arrived to the bewildered
Eva.

It was nature's last effort at comprehension; her mind was filled
with the one fatal knowledge—Cormac was gone for ever; and that
was the only mental consciousness that ever after employed the
lovely Eva.

The remainder of the melancholy tale is briefly told. Though
quite bereft of reason, she was harmless as a child, and was allowed
to wander round the borders of Lough Mask, and its immediate
neighbourhood. A favourite haunt of the still beautiful maniac was
the Cave of Cong, where a subterranean river rushes from beneath
a low natural arch in the rock, and passing for some yards over a
strand of pebbles, in pellucid swiftness, loses itself in the dark recesses
of the cavern with the sound of a rapid and turbulent fall. This river
is formed by the waters of Lough Mask becoming engulfed at one
of its extremities, and hurrying through a subterranean channel
until they rise again in the neighbourhood of Cong, and become
tributary to Lough Corrib. Here the poor girl would sit for hours;
and, believing that her beloved Cormac had been drowned in
Lough Mask, she hoped, in one of those half-intelligent dreams
which haunt a distempered brain, to arrest his body, as she fancied
it must pass through the Cave of Cong, borne on the subterranean
river.

Month after month passed by; but the nipping winter and the gentle spring found the lovely Eva still watching by the stream, like some tutelary water nymph beside her sacred fountain. At length she disappeared—and though the strictest search was made, the broken-hearted Eva was never heard of more; and the tradition of the country is, that the fairies took pity on a love so devoted, and carried away the faithful girl, to join her betrothed in fairy land!

Mrs ——— closed the manuscript, and replaced it in the little cabinet.

"Most likely," said I, "poor Eva, if ever such a person existed—"

"If!" said the fair reader. "Can you be so ungrateful as to question the truth of my legend, after all the trouble I have had in reading it to you? Get away! A sceptic like you is only fit to hear the commonplaces of the daily press."

"I cry your pardon, fair lady," said I. "I am most orthodox in legendary belief, and question not the existence of your Eva. I was only about to say that perchance she might have been drowned in, and carried away by, the river she watched so closely."

"Hush, hush," said the fair chronicler—"As you hope for favour or information in our fair counties of Galway or Mayo, never *dare* to question the truth of a legend—never venture a *'perhaps'* for the purpose of making a tale more reasonable, nor endeavour to substitute the reign of common sense, in hopes of superseding the empire of the fairies. Go to-morrow to the Cave of Cong, and if you return still an unbeliever, I give you up as an irreclaimable infidel."

1. The view from the Pass of Salruck in Cunnemara, commanding at once, on one side, the great Killery harbour, and on the other the Atlantic Ocean, once afforded me just such a magnificent prospect as the one described.

THE WHITE TROUT

A LEGEND OF CONG

Oh! I would ask no happier bed
Than the chill wave my love lies under
Sweeter to rest together, dead,
Far sweeter than to live asunder.

LALLA ROOKH

THE NEXT MORNING I PROCEEDED alone to the cave, to witness the natural curiosity of its subterranean river, my interest in the visit being somewhat increased by the foregoing tale. Leaving my horse at the little village of Cong, I bent my way on foot through the fields, if you may venture to give that name to the surface of this immediate district of the county Mayo, which, presenting large flat masses of limestone, intersected by patches of verdure, gives one the idea much more of a burial-ground covered with monumental slabs, than a formation of nature. Yet (I must make this remark *en passant*), such is the richness of the pasture in these little verdant interstices, that cattle are fattened upon it in a much shorter time than on a meadow of the most cultured aspect; and though to the native of Leinster, this *land* (if we may be pardoned a premeditated *bull*) would appear all *stones*, the Mayo farmer knows it from experience to be a profitable tenure. Sometimes deep clefts occur between these laminæ of limestone rock, which, closely overgrown with verdure, have not unfrequently occasioned serious accidents to man and beast; and one of these chasms, of larger dimensions than usual, forms the entrance to the celebrated cave in question. Very rude steps of unequal height, part natural and partly artificial, lead the explorer of its quiet beauty, by an abrupt descent, to the bottom of the cave, which contains an enlightened area of some thirty or forty feet, whence a naturally vaulted passage opens, of the deepest gloom. The depth of the cave may be about equal to its width at the bottom: the mouth is not more than twelve or fifteen feet across; and pendent from its margin clusters of ivy and other parasite plants hang and cling in all the fantastic variety of natural festooning and tracery. It is a truly beautiful and poetical little spot, and particularly interesting to the stranger, from being unlike any thing else one has ever seen, and having none of the noisy and vulgar pretence of regular *show-places*, which call upon you every moment to exclaim "Prodigious!"

An elderly and decent looking woman had just filled her pitcher with the deliciously cold and clear water of the subterranean river that flowed along its bed of small, smooth, and many-coloured pebbles, as I arrived at the bottom; and perceiving at once that I was a stranger, she paused, partly perhaps with the pardonable pride of displaying her local knowledge, but more from the native peasant politeness of her country, to become the temporary *Cicerone* of the cave. She spoke some words of Irish, and hurried forth on her errand a very handsome and active boy, of whom she informed me, she was the great-grandmother.

"Great-grandmother!" I repeated, in unfeigned astonishment.

"Yes, your honour," she answered, with evident pleasure sparkling in her eyes, which time had not yet deprived of their brightness, or the soul-subduing influence of this selfish world bereft of their kind-hearted expression.

"You are the youngest woman I have ever seen," said I, "to be a great-grandmother."

"Troth, I don't doubt you, Sir," she answered.

"And you seem still in good health, and likely to live many a year yet," said I.

"With the help of God, Sir," said she, reverently.

"But," I added, "I perceive a great number of persons about here of extreme age. Now, how long generally do the people in this country live?"

"Troth, Sir," said she, with the figurative drollery of her country, "we live here as long as we like."

"Well, that is no inconsiderable privilege," said I; "but you, nevertheless, must have married very young?"

"I was not much over sixteen, your honour, when I had my first child at my breast."

"That was beginning early," said I.

"Thrue for you, Sir; and faith, Noreen—(that's my daughter, Sir)—Noreen herself lost no time either; I suppose she thought she had as good a right as the mother before her—she was married at seventeen, and a likely couple herself and her husband was. So you see, Sir, it was not long before I was a granny. Well, to make the saying good, 'as the ould cock crows the young bird cherrups,' and faiks, the whole breed, seed, and generation, tuk after the owld woman (that's myself, Sir); and so, in coorse of time, I was not only a granny, but a *grate* granny and, by the same token, here comes my darling Paudeen Bawn,[1] with what I sent him for."

Here the fine little fellow I have spoken of, with his long fair hair curling about his shoulders, descended into the cave, bearing some faggots of bog-wood, a wisp of straw, and a lighted sod of turf.

"Now, your honour, it's what you'll see the pigeon-hole to advantage."

"What pigeon-hole?" said I.

"Here where we are," she replied.

"Why is it so called?" I inquired.

"Because, Sir, the wild pigeons often build in the bushes and the ivy that's round the mouth of the cave, and in here too," said she, pointing into the gloomy depth of the interior.

"Blow that turf, Paudeen;" and Paudeen, with distended cheeks and compressed lips, forthwith poured a few vigorous blasts on the sod of turf, which soon flickered and blazed, while the kind old woman lighted her faggots of bog-wood at the flame.

"Now, Sir, follow me," said my conductress.

"I am sorry you have had so much trouble on my account," said I.

"Oh, no throuble in life, your honour, but the greatest of pleasure;" and so saying, she proceeded into the cave, and I followed, carefully choosing my step by the help of her torch-light, along the slippery path of rock that overhung the river. When she had reached a point of some little elevation, she held up her lighted pine branches, and waving them to and fro, asked me could I see the top of the cave.

The effect of her figure was very fine, illumined as it was, in the mist of utter darkness, by the red glare of the blazing faggots; and as she wound them round her head, and shook their flickering sparks about, it required no extraordinary stretch of imagination to suppose her, with her ample cloak of dark drapery, and a few straggling tresses of grey hair escaping from the folds of a rather Eastern head-dress, some Sybil about to commence an awful rite, and evoke her ministering spirits from the dark void, or call some water demon from the river, which rushed unseen along, telling of its wild course by the turbulent dash of its waters, which the reverberation of the cave rendered still more hollow.

She shouted aloud and the cavern-echoes answered to her summons. "Look!" said she—and she lighted the wisp of straw, and flung it on the stream: it floated rapidly away, blazing in wild undulations over the perturbed surface of the river, and at length suddenly disappeared altogether. The effect was most picturesque and startling; it was even awful. I might almost say, sublime!

Her light being nearly expired, we retraced our steps, and emerging from the gloom, stood beside the river, in the enlightened area I have described.

"Now, Sir," said my old woman, "we must thry and see the White Throut; and you never seen a throut o' that colour yet, I warrant."

I assented to the truth of this.

"They say it's a fairy throut, your honour, and tells mighty quare stories about it."

"What are they?" I inquired.

"Troth, it's myself doesn't know the half o' them—only partly: but sthrive and see it before you go, Sir; for there's them that says it isn't lucky to come to the cave, and lave it without seem' the white throut; and if you're a bachelor, Sir, and didn't get a peep at it, throth you'd never be married; and sure that 'id be a murther?"[2]

"Oh," said I, "I hope the fairies would not be so spiteful—"

"Whisht—whisht!"[3] said she, looking fearfully around; then, knitting her brows, she gave me an admonitory look, and put her finger on her lip, in token of silence, and then coming sufficiently near me to make herself audible in a whisper, she said, "Never speak ill, your honour, of the good people—beyant all, in sitch a place as this—for it's in the likes they always keep; and one doesn't know who may be listenin'. God keep uz! But look, Sir! look!" And she pointed to the stream—"There she is."

"Who? what?" said I.

"The throut, Sir."

I immediately perceived the fish in question, perfectly a trout in shape, but in colour a creamy white, heading up the stream, and seeming to keep constantly within the region of the enlightened part of it.

"There it is, that very spot evermore," continued my guide, "and never any where else."

"The poor fish, I suppose, likes to swim in the light," said I.

"Oh, no, Sir," said she, shaking her head significantly, "the people here has a mighty owld story about that throut."

"Let me hear it, and you will oblige me."

"Och! it's only laughin' at me you'd be, and call me an ould fool, a the misthiss[4] beyant in the big house[5] often did afore, when she first kem among us—but she knows the differ now."

"Indeed I shall not laugh at your story," said I, "but on the contrary, shall thank you very much for your tale."

"Then sit down a minnit, Sir," said she, throwing her apron upon the rock, and pointing to the seat, "and I'll tell you to the best of my knowledge;" and seating herself on an adjacent patch of verdure, she began her legend.

"There was wanst upon a time, long ago, a beautiful young lady that lived in a castle up by the lake beyant, and they say she was promised to a king's son, and they wor to be married: when, all of a sudden, he was murthered, the crathur (Lord help us), and threwn into the lake above,[6] and so, of coorse, he couldn't keep his promise to the fair lady,—and more's the pity.

"Well, the story goes, that she went out iv her mind, bekase av loosin' the king's son—for she was tindher-hearted, God help her, like the rest iv us!—and pined away after him, until, at last, no one about seen her, good or bad; and the story wint, that the fairies took her away.

"Well, Sir, in coorse o' time, the white throut, God bless it, was seen in the sthrame beyant; and sure the people didn't know what to think av the crathur, seein' as how a white throut was never heerd av afore nor sence; and years upon years the throut was there, just where you seen it this blessed minit, longer nor I can tell—aye throth, and beyant the memory o' th' ouldest in the village.

"At last the people began to think it must be a fairy; for what else could it be?—and no hurt nor harm was iver put an the white throut, antil some wicked sinners of sojers[7] kem to these parts, and laughed at all the people, and gibed and jeered them for thinkin' o' the likes; and one o' them in partic'lar, (bad luck to him;—God forgi' me for sayin' it!) swore he'd catch the throut and ate it for his dinner—the blackguard!

"Well, what would you think o' the villiany of the sojer?—sure enough he cotch the throut; and away wid him home, and puts an the fryin'-pan, and into it he pitches the purty little thing. The throut squeeled all as one as Christian crathur, and, my dear, you'd think the sojer id split his sides laughin'—for he was a harden'd villian: and when he thought one side was done, he turns it over to fry the other; and what would you think, but the divil a taste of a burn was an it at all at all; and sure the sojer thought it was a *quare* throut that couldn't be briled; 'but,' says he, 'I'll give it another turn by and by'—little thinkin' what was in store for him, the haythen.

"Well, when he thought that side was done, he turns it again—and lo and behould you, the divil a taste more done that side was nor the other: 'Bad luck to me,' says the sojer, 'but that bates the world,' says he; 'but I'll thry you agin, my darlint,' says he, 'as cunnin' as you think yourself,'—and so, with that, he turns it over and over; but the divil a sign av the fire was an the purty throut. "Well,' says the desperate villian—(for sure, Sir, only he was a desperate villian *entirely*, he might know he was doin' a wrong thing, seein' that all his endayvours was no good); —'well,' says he, 'my jolly little throut, maybe you're fried enough, though you don't seem over-well dress'd; but you may be better than you look, like a singed cat, and a tit-bit, afther all,' says he; and with that he ups with his knife and fork to taste a piece o' the throut—but, my jew'l, the minit he puts his knife into the fish, there was a murtherin' screech, that you'd think the life id lave you if you heerd it, and away jumps the throut out av the fryin' pan into the middle o' the flure;[8] and an the spot where it fell, up riz[9] a lovely lady—the beautifullest young crathur that eyes ever seen, dressed in white, with a band o' goold in her hair, and a sthrame o' blood runnin' down her arm.

"'Look where you cut me, you villian,' says she, and she held out her arm to him— and, my dear, he thought the sight id lave his eyes.

"'Couldn't you lave me cool and comfortable in the river where you snared me, and not disturb me in my duty?' says she.

"'Well, he thrimbled like a dog in a wet sack, and at last he stammered out somethin,' and begged for his life, and ax'd her ladyship's pardin, and said he didn't know she was an duty, or he was too good a sojer not to know betther nor to meddle wid her.

"'I *was* on duty then,' says the lady; 'I was watchin' for my thru love, that is comin' by wather to me,' says she; 'an' if he comes while

I am away, an' that I miss iv him, I'll turn you into a pinkeen,[10] and I'll hunt you up and down for evermore, while grass grows or wather runs.'

"Well, the sojer thought the life id lave him, at the thoughts iv his bein' turned into a pinkeen and begged for marcy: and with that, says the lady—

"'Renounce your evil coorses,' says she, 'you villain, or you'll repint it too late; be a good man for the futhur, and go to your duty[11] reg'lar. And now,' says she, 'take me back, and put me into the river agin, where you found me.'

"'Oh, my lady,' says the sojer, 'how could I have the heart to drown a beautiful lady like you?'

"But before he could say another word, the lady was vanished, and there he saw the little throut an the ground. Well, he put it an a clane plate, and away he run for the bare life, for fear her lover would come while she was away; and he run, and he run, ever till he came to the cave agin, and threw the throut into the river. The minit he did, the wather was as red as blood for a little while, by rayson av the cut, I suppose, until the sthrame washed the stain away; and to this day thee's a little red mark an the throut's side, where it was cut.[12]

"Well, Sir, from that day out the sojer was an althered man, and reformed his ways, and wint to his duty reg'lar, and fasted three times a week—though it was never fish he tuk an fastin' days; for, afther the fright he got, fish id never rest an his stomach, God bless us—savin' your presence. But anyhow, he was an althered man, as I said before; and in coorse o' time he left the army, and turned hermit at last; and they say he *used to pray evermore for the sowl of the White Throut.*"

1.   Fair little Paddy.
2.   A great pity.
3.   Silence.
4.   The lady.

5. A gentleman's mansion.
6. Above.
7. Soldiers.
8. Floor.
9. Arose.
10. Stickle-back.
11. The Irish peasant calls his attendance at the confessional "going to his duty."
12. The fish has really a red spot on its side.

THE BATTLE
OF THE BERRINS

OR
THE DOUBLE FUNERAL

> Belong to the gallows, and be hanged, you rogue; is this a
> place to roar in? … Fetch me a dozen staves, and strong
> ones—these are but switches to them—I'll scratch your
> heads!

I WAS SITTING ALONE IN the desolate church-yard of ——, intent upon
my "silent art," lifting up my eyes from my portfolio, only to direct
them to the interesting ruin I was sketching—when the death-like
stillness that prevailed was broken by a faint and wild sound, unlike
any thing I had ever heard in my life. I confess I was startled—I paused
in my occupation, and listened in breathless expectation. Again this
seemingly unearthly sound vibrated through the still air of evening,
more audibly than at first, and partaking of the vibratory quality of
tone I have noticed, in so great a degree as to resemble the remote
sound of the ringing of many glasses crowded together.

I arose and looked around—no being was near me, and again
this heart-chilling sound struck upon my ear; its wild and wailing

intonation reminding me of the Æolian harp. Another burst was wafted up the hill; and then it became discernible that the sound proceeded from many voices raised in lamentation.

It was the *ulican*. I had hitherto known it only by report; for the first time, now, its wild and appalling cadence had ever been heard; and it will not be wondered at by those acquainted with it that I was startled on hearing it under such circumstances.

I could now perceive a crowd of peasants of both sexes, winding along a hollow way that led to the church-yard where I was standing, bearing amongst them the coffin of the departed; and ever and anon a wild burst of the *ulican* would arise from the throng, and ring in wild and startling *unison* up the hill, until, by a gradual and plaintive descent through an octave, it dropped into a subdued wail; and they bore the body onward the while, not in the measured and solemn step that custom (at least our custom) deems decent, but in a rapid and irregular manner, as if the violence of their grief hurried them on, and disdained all form.

The effect was certainly more impressive than that of any other funeral I had ever witnessed, however much the "pride, pomp, and circumstance," of such arrays had been called upon to produce a studied solemnity; for no hearse with sable plumes, nor chief mourners, nor pall-bearers, ever equalled in *poetry* or *picturesque* these poor people, bearing along on their shoulders, in the stillness of evening, the body of their departed friend to its "long home." The women raising their arms above their heads, in the untaught action of grief; their dark and ample cloaks waving wildly about, agitated by the varied motions of their wearers, and their wild cry raised in lament

   Most musical, most melancholy.

 At length they reached the cemetery, and the coffin was borne into the interior of the ruin, where the women still continued to wail for the dead, while half a dozen athletic young men immediately proceeded to prepare a grave; and seldom have I seen finer fellows, or men more full of activity; their action, indeed, bespoke so much life and vigour, as to induce an involuntary and melancholy contrast with the object on which that action was bestowed.

 Scarcely had the spade upturned the green sod of the burial-ground, when the wild peal of the *ulican* again was heard at a distance. The young men paused in their work, and turned their heads, as did all the bystanders towards the point whence the sound proceeded.

 We soon perceived another funeral procession wind round the foot of the hill, and immediately the grave-makers renewed their work with redoubled activity; while exclamations of anxiety on their part, for the completion of their work, and of encouragement from the lookers-on, resounded on all sides; and such ejaculations as "hurry, boys, hurry!"—"Stir yourself, Paddy!"—"That's your sort, Mike!"—"Rouse your sowl!" &c., &c., resounded on all sides. At the same time, the second funeral party that was advancing, no sooner perceived the church-yard already occupied, than they directly quickened their pace, as the wail rose more loudly and wildly from the train; and a detachment, bearing pick and spade, forthwith sallied from the main body, and dashed with headlong speed up the hill. In the mean time, an old woman, with streaming eyes and dishevelled hair, rushed wildly from the ruin where the first party had borne their coffin, towards the young athletes I have already described as working with "might and main," and addressing them with all the passionate intensity of her country, she exclaimed, "Sure you wouldn't let them have the advantage of uz, that-a-way, and lave my darlin' boy wanderin' about, dark an' 'lone in the long nights. Work, boys! work! for the bare life, and the mother's blessin' be an you, and let my poor Paudeen have rest."

I thought the poor woman was crazed, as indeed her appearance and vehemence of manner, as well as the (to me) unintelligible address she had uttered, might well induce me to believe, and I questioned one of the bystanders accordingly.

"An' is it why she's goin' wild about it, you're axin'?" said the person I addressed, in evident wonder at my question. "Sure then I thought all the world knew that, let alone a gintleman like you, that ought to be knowledgeable: and sure she doesn't want the poor boy to be walkin', as of coorse he must, barrin' they're smart."

"What do you mean?" said I, "I don't understand you."

"Whisht! whisht," said he; "here they come, by the powers, and the Gallaghers at the head of them," as he looked towards the new-comers' advanced-guard, who had now gained the summit of the hill, and, leaping over the boundary-ditch of the cemetery, advanced towards the group that surrounded the grave, with rapid strides and a resolute air.

"Give over there, I bid you," said a tall and ably-built man of the party, to those employed in opening the ground, who still plied their implements with energy.

"Give over, or it'll be worse for you. Didn't you hear me, Rooney?" said he, as he laid his muscular hand on the arm of one of the party he addressed, and arrested him in his occupation.

"I did hear you," said Rooney; "but I didn't heed you."

"I'd have you keep a civil tongue in your head," said the former.

"You're mighty ready to give advice that you want yourself," rejoined the latter, as he again plunged the spade into the earth.

"Lave off, I tell you!" said our Hercules, in a higher tone; "or, by this and that, I'll make you sorry!"

"Arrah! what brings you here at all?" said another of the grave-makers, "breedin' a disturbance?"

"What brings him here but mischief?" said a grey-haired man, who undertook, with national peculiarity, to answer one interrogatory by making another—"there's always a quarrel, whenever there's a Gallagher." For it was indeed one of "the Gallaghers" that the peasant I spoke to noticed as being "at the head o' them," who was assuming so bold a tone.

"You may thank your grey hairs, that I don't make you repent o' your words," said Gallagher, and his brow darkened as he spoke.

"Time was," said the old man, "when I had something surer than grey hairs to make such as you respect me;" and he drew himself up with an air of patriarchal dignity, and displayed in his still expansive chest and commanding height, the remains of a noble figure, that bore testimony to the truth of what he had just uttered. The old man's eye kindled as he spoke—but 'twas only for a moment; and the expression of pride and defiance was succeeded by that of coldness and contempt.

"I'd have beat you blind the best day ever you seen," said Gallagher, with an impudent swagger.

"Troth you wouldn't, Gallagher!" said a contemporary of the old man: "but your consait bates the world!"

"That's thrue," said Rooney. "He's a great man intirely, in his own opinion. I'd make a power of money if I could *buy* Gallagher at my price, and *sell* him at his *own.*'

A low and jeering laugh followed this hit of my friend Rooney; and Gallagher assumed an aspect so lowering, that a peasant standing near me, turned to his companion and said, significantly, "By gor, Ned, there'll be wig an the green afore long!"

And he was quite right.

The far-off speck on the horizon, whence the prophetic eye of a sailor can foretel the coming storm, is not more nicely discriminated by the mariner, than the symptoms of an approaching fray by an Irish man; and scarcely had the foregoing words been uttered, than I saw the men tucking up their long frieze coats in a sort of jacket fashion—thus getting rid of their *tails*, like game-cocks before a battle. A more menacing grip was taken by the bearer of each stick (a usual appendage of Hibernians); and a general closing-in of the bystanders round the nucleus of dissatisfaction, made it perfectly apparent that hostilities must soon commence.

I was not long left in suspense about such a catastrophe, for a general outbreaking soon took place, commencing in the centre with the principals already noticed, and radiating throughout the whole circle, until a general action ensued, and the belligerents were dispersed in various hostile groups over the churchyard.

I was a spectator from the topmost step of a stile leading into the burial-ground, deeming it imprudent to linger within the precincts of the scene of action, when my attention was attracted by the appearance of a horseman, who galloped up the little stony road, and was no sooner at my side, than he dismounted, exclaiming, at the top of his voice, "Oh! You reprobates, *lave* off, I tell you, you heathens! Are you Christians at all?"

I must here pause a moment to describe the person of the horseman in question. He was a tall, thin, pale man—having a hat, which from exposure to bad weather had its broad slouching brim crimped into many fantastic involutions—its crown somewhat depressed in the middle, and the edges of the same exhibiting a napless paleness; very far removed from its original black; no shirt-collar sheltered his angular jaw-bones—a narrow, white cravat was drawn tightly round his spare neck—a single-breasted coat of rusty black, with standing collar, was tightly buttoned nearly up to his chin, and a nether garment of the same, with large silver knee-buckles, meeting a square-cut and buckram-like pair of black leather boots, with heavy, plated spurs, that had seen the best of their days, completed the picture. His horse was a small, well-built hack, whose long rough coat would have been white, but that soiled litter had stained it to a dirty yellow; and taking advantage of the liberty which the abandoned rein afforded, he very quietly turned him to the little fringe of grass which bordered each side of the path, to make as much profit of his time as he might, before his rider at should resume his seat in the old high-pommelled saddle which he had vacated, in uttering the ejaculations I have recorded.

This person; then, hastily mounting the stile on which I stood, with rustic politeness said, "By your leave, Sir," as he pushed by me in haste, and jumping from the top of the wall, proceeded with long and rapid strides towards the combatants, and brandishing a heavy thong whip which he carried, he began to lay about him with equal vigour and impartiality on each and every of the peace-breakers, both parties sharing in the castigation thus bestowed, with the most even, and, I might add, *heavy*-handed justice.

My surprise was great on finding that all the blows inflicted by this new belligerent, instead of being resented by the assaulted parties, seemed taken as if resistance against this potent chastiser were vain, and in a short time they all fled before him, like so many frightened school-boys before an incensed pedagogue, and huddled themselves together in a crowd, which at once became pacified at his presence.

Seeing this result, I descended from my perch, and ran towards the scene that excited my surprise in no ordinary degree. I found this new-comer delivering to the multitude he had quelled, a severe reproof of their "unchristian doings," as he termed them; and it became evident that he was the pastor of the flock, and, it must be acknowledged, a very turbulent flock, he seemed to have of it.

This admonition was soon ended. It was certainly impressive, and well calculated for the audience to whom it was delivered of its language as the solemnity of its manner was much enhanced by the deep and somewhat sepulchral voice of the speaker. "And now," added the pastor, "let me ask you for what you were fighting like so many wild Indians; for surely your conduct is liker to savage creatures than men that have been bred up in the hearing of God's word?"

A pause of a few seconds followed this question; and, at length, some one ventured to answer from amongst the crowd, that it was "in regard of the berrin."

"And is not so solemn a sight," asked the priest, "as the burial of the departed, enough to keep down the evil passions of your hearts?"

"Troth then, and plaze your Riverince, it was nothin' ill-nathured in life, but only a good-nathured turn we wor doin' for poor Paudeen Mooney that's departed; and sure it's to your Riverence we'll be goin' immadiantly for the masses for the poor boy's sowl." Thus making interest in the offended quarter, with an address for which the Irish peasant is pre-eminently distinguished.

"Tut! tut!" rapidly answered the priest; anxious, perhaps, to silence this very palpable appeal to his own interest. "Don't talk to me about doing a good-natured turn. Not," added he, in a subdued under-tone, "but that prayers for the souls of the departed faithful are enjoined by the church; but what has that to do with your scandalous and lawless doings that I witnessed this minute? and you yourself," said he, addressing the last speaker, "one of the busiest with your alpeen? I'm afraid you're rather fractious, Rooney—take care that I don't speak to you from the altar."

"Oh, God forbid that your Riverince id have to do the like," said the mother of the deceased, already noticed, in an imploring tone, and with the big tear drops chasing each other down her cheeks; "and sure it was only they wanted to put my poor boy in the ground *first,* and no wondher sure, as your Riverince *knows,* and not to have my poor Paudeen—"

"Tut! tut! woman," interrupted the priest, waving his hand rather impatiently, "don't let me hear any folly."

"I ax your Riverince's pardon, and sure it's myself that id be sorry to offind my clargy—God's blessin' be an them night and day! But I was only goin' to put in a word for Mikee Rooney, and sure it wasn't him at all, nor wouldn't be any of us, only for Shan Gallagher, that wouldn't lave us in peace."

"Gallagher!" said the priest, in a deeply-reproachful tone. "Where is he?"

Gallagher came not forward, but the crowd drew back, and left him revealed to the priest. His aspect was that of sullen indifference and he seemed to be the only person present totally uninfluenced by the presence of his pastor, who now advanced towards him, and extending his attenuated hand in the attitude of denunciation towards the offender, said very solemnly—

"I have already spoken to you in the house of worship, and now, once more, I warn you to beware. Riot and battle are found wherever you go, and if you do not speedily reform your course of life, I shall expel you from the pale of the church, and pronounce sentence of excommunication upon you from the altar."

Every one appeared awed by the solemnity and severity of this address from the onset, but when the word "excommunication" was uttered, a thrill of horror seemed to run through the assembled multitude: and even Gallagher himself I thought betrayed some emotion on hearing the terrible word. Yet he evinced it but for a moment, and turning on his heel, he retired from the ground with something of the swagger with which he entered it. The crowd opened to let him pass and opened widely, as if they sought to avoid contact with one so fearfully denounced.

"You have two coffins here," said the clergyman, "proceed, therefore, immediately to make two graves, and let the bodies be interred at the same time, and I will read the service for the dead."

No very great time was consumed in making the necessary preparation. The "narrow beds" were made, and, as their tenants were consigned to their last long sleep, the solemn voice of the priest was raised in the "De Profundis;" and when he had concluded the short and beautiful psalm, the friends of the deceased closed the graves, and covered them neatly with fresh-cut sods, which is what *Paddy* very metaphorically calls

Putting the daisy quilt over him.

The clergyman retired from the church-yard, and I followed his footsteps for the purpose of introducing myself to "his reverence," and seeking from him an explanation of what was still a most unfathomable mystery to me, namely the cause of the quarrel, which, from certain passages in his address to the people, I saw he understood, though so slightly glanced at. Accordingly, I overtook the priest, and as the Irish song has it,

To him I obnoxiously made my approaches.

He received me with courtesy, which though not savouring much of intercourse with polished circles, seemed to spring whence all true politeness emanates—from a good heart.

I begged to assure him it was not an impertinent curiosity which made me desirous of becoming acquainted with the cause of the fray which I had witnessed, and he had put a stop to in so summary a manner; and hoped he would not consider it an intrusion if I applied to him for that purpose.

"No intrusion in life, Sir," answered the priest very frankly, and with a rich brogue, whose intonation was singularly expressive of good nature. It was the specimen of brogue I have never met but in one class, the Irish gentleman of the last century—an accent, which, though it possessed all the characteristic traits of "the brogue," was at the same time divested of the slightest trace of vulgarity. This is not to be met with now, or at least very rarely. An attempt has been made by those who fancy it genteel, to graft the English accent upon the Broguish stem—and a very bad fruit it has produced. The truth is, the accents of the two countries could never be happily blended; and far from making a pleasing amalgamation, it conveys the idea that the speaker is endeavouring to *escape* from his own accent for what he considers a superior one; and it is this attempt to be fine, which so particularly allies the idea of vulgarity with the tone of brogue so often heard in the present day.

Such, I have said, was *not* the brogue of the Rev. Phelim Roach, or Father Roach, as the peasants called him; and his voice, which I have earlier noticed as almost sepulchral, I found derived that character from the feeling of the speaker when engaged in an admonitory address; for when employed on colloquial occasions, it was no more than what might be called a rich and deep manly voice. So much for Father Roach, who forthwith proceeded to enlighten me on the subject of the funeral, and the quarrel arising therefrom.

"The truth is, Sir, these poor people are possessed of many foolish superstitions; and however we may, as *men*, pardon them, looking upon them as fictions originating in a warm imagination, and finding a ready admission into the minds of an unlettered and susceptible peasantry, we cannot, as pastors of the flock, admit their belief to the poor people committed to our care."

This was quite new to me; to find a clergyman of the religion I had hitherto heard of as being *par excellence* abounding in superstition, denouncing the very article in question.—But let me not interrupt Father Roach.

"The superstition I speak of," continued he, "is one of the many these warm-hearted people indulge in, and is certainly very poetical in its texture.

"But, Sir," interrupted my newly-made acquaintance, pulling forth a richly chased gold watch of antique workmanship, that at once suggested ideas of the '*bon vieux temps*,' "I must ask your pardon—I have an engagement to keep at the little hut I call my home, which obliges me to proceed there forthwith. If you have so much time to spare as will enable you to talk with me to the end of this little road, it will suffice to make you acquainted with the nature of the superstition in question."

I gladly assented; and the priest, disturbing the nibbling occupation of his hack, threw the rein over his arm, and the docile little beast following him on one side as quietly as I did on the other, he gave me the following account of the cause of all the previous riot, as we wound down the little stony path that led to the main road.

"There is a belief among the peasantry in this particular district, that the ghost of the last person interred in the church-yard, is obliged to traverse, unceasingly, the road between this earth and purgatory, carrying water to slake the burning thirst of those confined in that 'limbo large;' and that the ghost is thus obliged to walk

Through the dead waste and middle of the night,

until some fresh arrival of a tenant to the 'narrow house,' supplies a fresh ghost to 'relieve guard,' if I may be allowed so military an expression; and thus, the supply of water to the sufferers in purgatory is kept up unceasingly."[1]

Hence it was that the fray had arisen, and the poor mother's invocation, "that her darling boy should not be left to wander about the church-yard dark and lone in the long nights," became at once intelligible. Father Roach gave me some curious illustrations of the different ways in which this superstition influenced his "poor people," as he constantly called them; but I suppose my readers have had quite enough of the subject, and I shall therefore say no more of other "cases in point," contented with having given them one example, and recording the existence of a superstition, which, however wild, undoubtedly owes its existence to an affectionate heart and a poetic imagination.

1. A particularly affectionate husband, before depositing the remains of his departed wife in the grave, placed a pair of new brogues in her coffin, that she might not have to walk all the way to purgatory barefooted. This was vouched for as a fact.

FATHER ROACH

I FOUND THE COMPANY OF Father Roach so pleasant, that I accepted an invitation which he gave me, when we arrived at the termination of our walk, to breakfast the next morning at the little hut, as he called the unpretending but neat cottage he inhabited, a short mile distant from the church-yard where we first met. I repaired, accordingly, the next morning, at an early hour, to my appointment, and found the worthy pastor ready to receive me. He met me at the little avenue, (not that I mean to imply an idea of grandeur by the term), which led from the main road to his dwelling—it was a short narrow road, bordered on each side by alder bushes, and an abrupt awkward turn placed you in front of the humble dwelling of which he was master; the area before it, however, was clean, and the offensive dunghill, the intrusive pig, and barking cur-dog, were not the distinguishing features of this as unfortunately they too often are of other Irish cottagers.

On entering the house, an elderly and comfortably-clad woman curtsied as we crossed the threshold, and I was led across an apartment, whose

> Neatly sanded floor—

(an earthen one, by the way)—we traversed diagonally to an opposite corner, where an open door admitted us into a small but comfortable boarded apartment, where breakfast was laid, unostentatiously but neatly, and inviting to the appetite, as far as that could be stimulated by a white cloth, most promising fresh butter, a plate of evidently fresh eggs, and the best of cream, whose rich white was most advantageously set off by the plain blue ware of which the ewer was composed; add to this, an ample cake of fresh griddle bread, and

> Though last, not least,

the savoury smell that arose from a rasher of bacon, which announced itself through the medium of more senses than one; for its fretting and fuming in the pan, playing many an ingenious variation upon "fiz and whiz!"

> Gave dreadful note of preparation.

But I must not forget to notice the painted tin tea canister of mine host which was emblazoned with the talismanic motto of

> "O'Connell and Liberty;"

and underneath the semicircular motto aforesaid, appeared the rubicund visage of a lusty gentleman in a green coat, holding in his hands a scroll inscribed with the dreadful words, "Catholic rent,"

> "Unpleasing most to Brunswick ears,"

which was meant to represent no less a personage than the "Great Liberator" himself.

While breakfast was going forward, the priest and myself had made no inconsiderable advances towards intimacy. Those who have mingled much in the world, have often, no doubt, experienced like myself, how much easier it is to enter at once, almost, into friendship with some, before the preliminaries of common acquaintance can be established with others.

Father Roach was one of the former species. We soon sympathised with each other; and becoming, as it were, at once possessed of the keys of each other's freemasonry, we mutually unlocked our confidence. This led to many an interesting conversation with the good father, while I remained in his neighbourhood. He gave me a sketch of his life in a few words. It was simply this: he was a descendant of a family that had once been wealthy and of large possessions in the very county, where, as he said himself, he was "a pauper."

"For what else can I call himself," said the humble priest, "when I depend on the gratuitous contributions of those who are little better than paupers themselves, for my support? But God's will be done."

His forefathers had lost their patrimony by repeated forfeitures, under every change of power that had distracted the unfortunate island of which he was a native;[1] and for him and his brothers, nothing was left but personal exertion.

"The elder boys would not remain here," said he, "where their religion was a barrier to their promotion. They went abroad, and offered their swords to the service of a foreign power. They fought and fell under the banner of Austria, who disdained not the accession of all such strong arms and bold hearts, that left their native soil to be better appreciated in a stranger land.

"I, and a younger brother, who lost his father ere he could feel the loss, remained in poor Ireland. I was a sickly boy, and was constantly near my beloved mother—rest her soul!—who early instilled into my infant mind, deeply reverential notions of which at length imbued my mind so strongly wit their influence, that I determined to devote my life to the priesthood. I was sent to St Omer to study, and on my return was appointed to the ministry, which I have ever since exercised to the best of the ability that God has vouchsafed to his servant."

Such was the outline of Father Roach's personal and family history.

In some of the conversations which our intimacy originated, I often sought for information, touching the peculiar doctrine of his church, and the discipline which its followers are enjoined to adapt.

I shall not attempt to weary the reader with an account of our arguments; for the good Father Roach was so meek as to condescend to an argument with one unlearned as myself, and a heretic to boot; nor to detail some anecdotes that to me were interesting on various points in question. I shall reserve but *one fact*—and a most singular one it is—to present to my readers on the subject of confession.

Speaking upon this point, I remarked to Father Roach, that of all the practices of the Roman Catholic Church, that of confession I considered the most beneficial within the range of its discipline.

He concurred with me in admitting it as highly advantageous to the sinner. I ventured to add that I considered it very beneficial also to the person sinned against.

"Very true," said Father Roach; "restitution is often made through its agency."

"But in higher cases than those you allude to," said I; "for instance, the detection of conspiracies, unlawful meetings, &c., &c."

"Confession," said he, somewhat hesitatingly, "does not immediately come into action in the way you allude to."

I ventured to hint, rather cautiously, that in this kingdom, where the Roman Catholic religion was not the one established by law, that there might be some reserve between penitent and confessor, on a subject where the existing government might be looked upon something in the light of a stepmother.[2]

A slight flush pass d over the priest's pallid face—"No, no," said he; 'do not suspect us of any foul play to the power under which we live.—No!—But recollect, the doctrine of our church is this—that whatsoever penance may be enjoined on the offending penitent by his confession, his crime, however black, must in all cases be held sacred, when its acknowledgment is made under the seal of confession."

"In all cases?" said I.

"Without an exception," answered he.

"Then, would you feel it your duty to give a murderer up to justice?"

The countenance of Father Roach assumed an instantaneous change, as if a sudden pang shot through him—his lip became suddenly ashy pale, he hid his face in his hands, and seemed struggling with some deep emotion. I fear I had offended, and feeling quite confused, began to stammer out some nonsense, when he interrupted me.

"Do not be uneasy," said he. "You have said nothing to be ashamed of, but your words touched a chord," and his voice trembled as he spoke, "that cannot vibrate without intense pain;" and wiping away a tear that glistened in each humid eye, "I shall tell you a story," said he, "that will be the strongest illustration of such a case as you have supposed;"—and he proceeded to give me the following narrative.

1. This has been too often the case in Ireland. Separated as the country is from the seat of government, it is only lately that the interests of Ireland have been an object to Great Britain. To say nothing of the earlier oppressions and confiscations, the adherents of the first Charles in Ireland were crushed by Cromwell. The forfeitures under the Commonwealth were tremendous.—"Hell or Connaught," still lives as a proverb. Charles II was not careful to repair the wrongs which his subjects suffered for being adherents of his father; and yet their loyalty remained unshaken to the faithless race, in the person of the second James. A new series of forfeitures then ensued under William the Third; and thus, by degrees, the principal ancient families of Ireland had their properties wrested from them, and bestowed upon the troopers of successive invaders; and for what?—attachment to the kings to whom they had sworn allegiance. The Irish have been, most unjustly, often denominated rebels. We shall find the truth is, if we consult history, their great misfortune has been, that they were only *too loyal*. But England is, at length, desirous of doing Ireland justice.

2. This was previously to the passing of the Roman Catholic relief bill.

THE PRIEST'S STORY

"I HAVE ALREADY MADE MYSELF known unto you, that a younger brother and myself were left to the care of my mother—best and dearest of mothers!" said the holy man, sighing deeply, and clasping his hands fervently, while his eyes were lifted to heaven, as if love made him conscious that the spirit of her he lamented had found its eternal rest there—"thy gentle and affectionate nature sunk under the bitter trial that an all-wise providence was pleased to visit thee with!—Well, sir, Frank was my mother's darling; not that you are to understand, by so saying, that she was of that weak and capricious tone of mind which lavished its care upon one at the expense of others—far from it: never was a deep store of maternal love more equally shared than among the four brothers; but when the two seniors went away, and I was some time after sent, for my studies, to St Omer, Frank became the object upon which all the tenderness of her affectionate heart might exercise the little maternal cares, that hitherto had been divided amongst many. Indeed, my dear Frank deserved it all; his was the gentlest of natures combined with a mind of singular strength and brilliant imagination. In short, as the phrase has it, he was 'the flower of the flock,' and great things were expected from him. It was sometime after my return from St Omer, while preparations were making for advancing Frank in the pursuit which had been selected as the business of his life, that every hour which drew nearer to the moment of his departure made him dearer, not only to us, but to all who knew him, and each

friend claimed a day that Frank should spend with him, which always passed in recalling the happy hours they had already spent together, in assurances given and received of kindly remembrances that still should be cherished, and in mutual wishes for success, with many a hearty prophecy from my poor Frank's friends, 'that he would one day be a great man.'

One night, as my mother and myself were sitting at home beside the fire, expecting Frank's return from one of these parties, my mother said, in an unusually anxious tone, 'I wish Frank was come home.'"

"What makes you think of his return so soon?" said I.

"'I don't know,' said she; 'but somehow, I'm uneasy about him.'

"'Oh, make yourself quiet,' said I, 'on that subject; we cannot possibly expect Frank for an hour to come yet.'

Still my mother could not become calm, and she fidgeted about the room, became busy in doing nothing, and now would go to the door of the house to listen for the distant tramp of Frank's horse; but Frank came not.

"More than the hour I had named, as the probable time of his return had elapsed, and my mother's anxiety had amounted to a painful pitch; and I began myself to blame my brother for so long and late an absence. Still, I endeavoured to calm her, and had prevailed on her to seat herself again at the fire, and commenced reading a page or two of an amusing book, when, suddenly she stopped me, and turned her head to the window in the attitude of listening.

"'It is! it is!' said she; 'I hear him coming.'

"And now the sound of a horse's feet in a rapid pace became audible. She rose from her chair, and with a deeply aspirated 'Thank God!' went to open the door for him herself. I heard the horse now pass by the window; in a second or two more, the door was opened, and instantly a fearful scream from my mother brought me hastily to her assistance. I found her lying in the hall in a deep swoon—the servants of the house hastily crowded to the spot, and gave her immediate aid. I ran to the door to ascertain the cause of my mother's alarm, and there I saw Frank's horse panting and foaming, and the saddle empty. That my brother had been thrown and badly hurt, was the first thought that suggested itself; and a car and horse were immediately ordered to drive in the direction he had been returning; but, in a few minutes, our fears were excited to the last degree, by discovering there was blood on the saddle.

We all experienced inconceivable terror at the discovery, but, not to weary you with details, suffice it to say, that we commenced a diligent search, and at length arrived at a small by-way that turned from the main road, and led through a bog, which was the nearest course for my brother to have taken homewards, and we accordingly began to explore it. I was mounted on the horse my brother had ridden, and the animal snorted violently, and exhibited evident symptoms of dislike to retrace this by-way, which, I doubted not, he had already travelled that night; and this very fact made me still more apprehensive that some terrible occurrence must have taken place. to occasion such excessive repugnance on the part of the animal. However, I urged him onward, and telling those who accompanied me, to follow with what speed they might, I dashed forward, followed by a faithful dog of poor Frank's. At the termination of about half a mile, the horse became still more impatient of restraint, and started at every ten paces; and the dog began to traverse the little road, giving an occasional yelp, sniffing the air strongly, and lashing his sides with his tail, as if on some scent. At length he came to a stand, and beat about within a very circumscribed space—yelping occasionally, as if to draw my attention. I dismounted immediately, but the horse was so extremely restless, that the difficulty I had in holding him prevented me from observing the road by the light of the lantern which I carried. I perceived, however, it was very much trampled hereabouts, and bore evidence of having been the scene of a struggle. I shouted to the party in the rear, who soon came up and lighted some faggots of bog-wood which they brought with them to assist in our search, and we now more clearly distinguished the marks I have alluded to. The dog still howled, and indicated a particular spot to us; and on one side of the path, upon the stunted grass, we discovered a quantity of fresh blood, and I picked up a pencil case that I knew had belonged to my murdered brother—for I now was compelled to consider him as such; and an attempt to describe the agonised feelings which at that moment I experienced would be in vain. We continued our search for the discovery of his body for many hours without success, and the morning was far advanced before we returned home. How changed a home from the preceding day! My beloved mother could scarcely be roused for a moment from a sort of stupor that seized upon her, when the paroxysm of frenzy was over, which the awful catastrophe of the fatal night had produced. If ever heart was broken, hers was. She lingered but a few weeks after the son she adored, and seldom spoke during the period, except to call upon his name.

"But I will not dwell on this painful theme. Suffice it to say—she died; and her death, under such circumstances, increased the sensation which my brother's mysterious murder had excited. Yet, with all the horror which was universally entertained for the crime, and the execrations poured upon its atrocious perpetrator, still, the doer of the deed remained undiscovered! and even I, who of course was the most active in seeking to develop the mystery, not only could catch no clue to lead to the discovery of the murderer, but failed even to ascertain where the mangled remains of my lost brother had been deposited.

"It was nearly a year after the fatal event, that a penitent knelt to me, and confided to the ear of his confessor the misdeeds of an ill-spent life; I say of his whole life—for he had never before knelt at the confessional.

"Fearful was the catalogue of crime that was revealed to me—unbounded selfishness, oppression, revenge, and lawless passion, had held unbridled influence over the unfortunate sinner, and sensuality in all its shapes, even to the polluted home and betrayed maiden, had plunged him deeply into sin.

"I was shocked—I may even say I was disgusted, and the culprit himself seemed to shrink from the recapitulation of his crimes, which he found more extensive and appalling than he had dreamed of, until the recital of them called them all up in fearful array before him. I was about to commence an admonition, when he interrupted me—he had more to communicate. I desired him to proceed—he writhed before me. I enjoined him in the name of the God he had offended, and who knoweth the inmost heart, to make an unreserved disclosure of his crimes, before he dared to seek a reconciliation with his Maker. At length, after many a pause and convulsive sob, he told me, in a voice almost suffocated by terror, that he had been guilty of bloodshed. I shuddered, but in a short time I recovered myself, and asked how and where he had deprived a fellow-creature of life? Never, to the latest hour of my life, shall I forget the look which the miserable sinner gave me at that moment. His eyes were glazed, and seemed starting from their sockets with terror; his face assumed a deadly paleness—he raised his clasped hands up to me in the most imploring action, as if supplicating mercy, and with livid and quivering lips he gasped out—''Twas I who killed your brother!'

"Oh God! how I felt at that instant! Even now, after the lapse of years, I recollect the sensation: it was as if the blood were flowing back upon my heart, until I felt as if it would burst; and then, a few convulsive breathings,—and back rushed the blood again through my tingling veins. I thought I was dying; but suddenly I uttered an hysteric laugh, and fell back, senseless, in my seat.

"When I recovered, a cold sweat was pouring down my forehead, and I was weeping copiously. Never, before, did I feel my manhood annihilated under the influence of an hysterical affection—it was dreadful.

"I found the bloodstained sinner supporting me, roused from his own prostration by a sense of terror at my emotion; for when I could hear any thing, his entreaties that I would not discover upon him, were poured forth in the most abject strain of supplication. 'Fear not for your miserable life,' said I; 'the seal of confession is upon what you have revealed to me, and so far you are safe, but leave me for the present, and come not to me again until I send for you.'—He departed.

"I knelt and prayed for strength to Him who alone could give it, to fortify me in this dreadful trial. Here was the author of a brother's murder, and a mother's consequent death, discovered to me in the person of my penitent. It was a fearful position for a frail mortal to be placed in but as a consequence of the holy calling I professed, I hoped, through the blessing of Him whom I served, to acquire fortitude for the trial into which the ministry of his gospel had led me.

"The fortitude I needed came through prayer, and when I thought myself equal to the task, I sent for the murderer of my brother. I officiated for him as our church has ordained—I appointed penances to him, and, in short, dealt with him merely as any other confessor might have done.

"Years thus passed away, and during that time he constantly attended his duty; and it was remarked through the country, that he had become a quieter person since Father Roach had become his confessor. But still he was not liked—and indeed, I fear he was far from a reformed man, though he did not allow his transgressions to be so glaring as they were wont to be; and I began to think that terror and cunning had been his motives in suggesting to him the course he had adopted, as the opportunities which it gave him of being often with me as his confessor, were likely to lull every suspicion of his guilt in the eyes of the world; and in making me the depositary of his fearful secret, he thus placed himself beyond the power of my pursuit, and interposed the strongest barrier to my becoming the avenger of his bloody deed.

"Hitherto I have not made you acquainted with the cause of that foul act—it was jealousy. He found himself rivalled by my brother in the good graces of a beautiful girl of moderate circumstances, whom he would have wished to obtain as his wife, but to whom Frank had become an object of greater interest; and I doubt not, had my poor fellow been spared, that marriage would ultimately have drawn closer the ties that were so savagely severed. But the ambuscade and the knife had done their deadly work; for the cowardly villain had lain in wait for him on the lonely bog-road he guessed he would travel on that fatal night,—and, springing from his lurking-place, he stabbed my noble Frank in the back.

"Well, Sir, I fear I am tiring you with a story which, you cannot wonder, is interesting to me; but I shall hasten to a conclusion.

"One gloomy evening in March, I was riding along the very road where my brother had met his fate, in company with his murderer. I know not what brought us together in such a place, except the hand of Providence, that sooner or later brings the murderer to justice; for I was not wont to pass the road, and loathed the company of the man who happened to overtake me upon it. I know not whether it was some secret visitation of conscience that influenced him at the time, or that he thought the lapse of years had wrought upon me so far as to obliterate the grief for my brother's death, which had never been, till that moment alluded to, however remotely, since he confessed his crime. Judge then my surprise, when, directing my attention to a particular point in the bog, he said,

"''Tis close by the place that your brother is buried.'

"I could not, I think, have been more astonished had my brother appeared before me.

"'What brother?' said I.

"'Your brother Frank,' said he; ''twas there I buried him, poor fellow, after I killed him.'

"'Merciful God!' I exclaimed, 'thy will be done,' and seizing the rein of the culprit's horse, I said, 'Wretch that you are! you have owned to the shedding of the innocent blood that has been crying to heaven for vengeance these ten years, and I arrest you here as my prisoner.'

"He turned ashy pale, as he faltered out a few words, to say I had promised not to betray him.

"'"Twas under the seal of confession,' said I, 'that you disclosed the deadly secret, and under that seal my lips must have been for ever closed but now, even in the very place where your crime was committed, it has pleased God that you should arraign yourself in the face of the world—and the brother of your victim is appointed to be the avenger of his innocent blood.'

"He was overwhelmed by the awfulness of this truth, and unresistingly he rode beside me to the adjacent town of ——, where he was committed for trial.

"The report of this singular and providential discovery of a murder excited a great deal of interest in the country; and as I was known to be the culprit's confessor, the bishop of the diocese forwarded a statement to a higher quarter, which procured for me a dispensation as regarded the confessions of the criminal; and I was handed this instrument, absolving me from further secrecy, a few days before the trial. I was the principal evidence against the prisoner. The body of my brother had, in the interim, been found in the spot his murderer had indicated, and the bog preserved it so far from decay, as to render recognition a task of no difficulty; the proof was so satisfactorily adduced to the jury, that the murderer was found guilty and executed, ten years after he had committed the crime.

"The judge pronounced a very feeling comment on the nature of the situation in which I had been placed for so many years; and passed a very flattering eulogium upon what he was pleased to call, 'my heroic observance of the obligation of secrecy by which I had been bound.'

"Thus, Sir, you see how sacred a trust that of a fact revealed under confession is held by our church, when even the avenging a brother's murder was not sufficient warranty for its being broken."[1]

1.   This story is a fact, and the comment of the judge upon the priest's fidelity, I am happy to say, is true.

THE KING AND THE BISHOP

A LEGEND OF CLONMACNOISE

Guildenstern—The King, Sir,—
Hamlet—Ay, Sir, what of him?
Guil.— Is, in his retirement, marvellously distempered.
Ham.—With drink, Sir?
Guil.—No, my Lord.

THERE ARE FEW THINGS MORE pleasant to those who are doomed to pass the greater part of their lives in the dust, and din, and smoke of a city, than to get on the top of a stage-coach, early some fine summer morning, and whirl along through the yet unpeopled streets, echoing from their emptiness to the rattle of the welcome wheels that are bearing you away from your metropolitan prison, to the

Free blue streams and the laughing sky

of the sweet country. How gladly you pass the last bridge over one of the canals—and then, deeming yourself fairly out of town, you look back once only on its receding "groves of chimneys," and, settling yourself comfortably in your seat, you cast away care, and look forward in gleeful anticipation of your three or four weeks in the tranquillity and freedom of a country ramble.

Such have my sensations often been; not a little increased, by the by, as I hugged closer to my side my portfolio, well stored with paper, and heard the rattle of my pencils and colours in the tin sketching box in my pocket. Such were they when last I started one fresh and lovely summer's morning, on the Ballinasloe coach, and promised myself a rich treat in a visit to Clonmacnoise, or "the churches," as the place is familiarly called by the peasantry.—Gladly I descended from my lofty station on our dusty conveyance, when it arrived at Shannonbridge, and engaging a boat, embarked on the noble river whence the village takes its name, and proceeded up the wide and winding stream, to the still sacred and once celebrated Clonmacnoise, the second monastic foundation established in Ireland, once tenanted by the learned and the powerful, now scarcely known but to the mendicant pilgrim, the learned antiquary, or the vagrant lover of the picturesque.

Here, for days together, have I lingered, watching its noble "ivy-mantled" tower, reposing in shadow, or sparkling in sunshine, as it spired upward in bold relief against the sky; or admiring the graceful involutions of the ample Shannon that wound beneath the gentle acclivity on which I stood, through the plashy meadows and the wide waste of bog, whose rich brown tones of colour faded into blue on the horizon; or in noting the red-tanned sail of some passing turf-boat, as it broke the monotony of the quiet river, or in recording with my pencil the noble stone cross, or the tracery of some mouldering ruin,

> Where ivied arch, or pillar lone,
> Plead haughtily for glories gone,

though I should not say "haughtily," for poor old Clonmacnoise pleads with as much humility as the religion which reared her now does; and which, like her, interesting in the attitude of decay, teaches and appeals to our sympathies and our imagination, instead of taking the strongholds of our reason by storm, and forcing our assent by overwhelming batteries of irrefragable proof, before it seeks to win our will by tender and impassioned appeals to the heart. But I wander from Clonmacnoise. It is a truly solemn and lonely spot; I love it almost to a folly, and have wandered day after day through its quiet cemetery, till I have almost made acquaintance with its ancient grave-stones.

One day I was accosted by a peasant who had watched for a long time, in silent wonder, the draft of the stone cross, as it grew into being beneath my pencil; and finding the man "apt," as the ghost says to Hamlet, I entered into conversation with him. To some remark of mine touching the antiquity of the place, he assured me "it was a fine *ould* place, in the *ould* ancient times." In noticing the difference between the two round towers, for there are *two* very fine ones at Clonmacnoise, one on the top of the hill, and one close beside the plashy bank of the river, he accounted for the difference by a piece of legendary information with which he favoured me, and which may, perhaps, prove of sufficient importance to interest the reader.

"You see, Sir," said he, "the one down there beyant, at the river side, was built the first, and finished complate entirely, for the roof is an it, you see; but when that was built, the bishop thought that another id look very purty on the hill beyant, and so he bid the masons set to work, and build up another tower there.

"Well, away they went to work, as busy as nailers; troth it was jist like a bee-hive, every man with his hammer in his hand, and sure the tower was complated in due time. Well, when the last stone was laid on the roof, the bishop axes the masons how much he was to pay them, and they ups and towld him their price; but the bishop, they say, was a neygar (niggard), God forgi' me for saying the word of so holy a man! and he said they axed too much, and he wouldn't pay them. With that, my jew'l, the masons said they would take no less; and what would you think, but the Bishop had the cunnin' to take away the ladthers that was reared up agin the tower.

"'And now,' says he, 'my gay fellows,' says he, 'the divil a down out o' that you'll come antil you larn manners, and take what's offered to yees,' says he; 'and when yees come down in your price you may come down yourselves into the bargain.'

"Well, sure enough he kep his word, and wouldn't let man nor mortyel nigh them to help them; and faiks the masons didn't like the notion of losing their honest airnins, and small blame to them; but sure they wor starvin' all the time, and didn't know what in the wide world to do when there was a fool chanc'd to pass by, and seen them.

"'Musha! but you look well there,' says the innocent, 'an' how are you?' says he.

"'Not much the betther av your axin,' says they.

"'Maybe you're out there,' says he. So he questioned them, and they tould him how it was with them, and how the bishop tuk away the ladthers, and they couldn't come down.

"'Tut, you fools,' says he, 'sure isn't it aiser to take down two stones nor to put up one?'

"Wasn't that mighty cute o' the fool, sir? And wid that, my dear sowl, no sooner said than done. Faiks the masons began to pull down their work, and whin they went an for some time, the bishop bid them stop, and he'd let them down; but faiks, before he gev in to them they had taken the roof clane off; and that's the raison that one tower has a roof, Sir, and the other has none."

But before I had seen Clonmacnoise and its towers, I was intimate with the most striking of its legends by favour of the sinewy boatman who rowed me to it. We had not long left Shannonbridge, when, doubling an angle of the shore, and stretching up a reach of the river where it widens, the principal round tower of Clonmacnoise became visible.

"What tower is that?" said I to my Charon.

"That's the big tower of Clonmacnoise, Sir," he answered; "an', if your honour looks sharp a little to the right of it, lower down, you'll see the ruins of the ould palace."

On a somewhat closer inspection, I did perceive the remains he spoke of, dimly discernible in the distance; and it was not without his indication of their relative situation to the tower, that I could have distinguished them from the sober grey of the horizon behind them, for the evening was closing fast, and we were moving eastward.

"Does your honour see it yit?" said my boatman.

"I do," said I.

"God spare you your eye-sight," responded he, "for troth it's few gintlemen could see the ould palace this far off, and the sun so low, barrin' they were used to *sportin'*, and had a sharp eye for the birds over a bog, or the like o' that. Oh, then it's Clonmacnoise, your honour, that's the holy place," continued he: "mighty holy in the ould ancient times, and mighty great too, wid the sivin churches, let alone the two towers, and the bishop, and plinty o' priests, and all to that.

"Two towers?" said I; "then I suppose one has fallen?"

"Not at all, Sir," said he; "but the other one that you can't see, is beyant in the hollow by the river side."

"And it was a great place, you say, in the *ould ancient times?*"

"Troth it was, Sir, and is still, for to this day it *bates* the world in regard o' pilgrims."

"Pilgrims!" I ejaculated.

"Yes, Sir," said the boatman, with his own quiet manner; although it was evident to a quick observer, that my surprise at the mention of pilgrims had not escaped him.

I mused a moment. Pilgrims, thought I, in the *British* dominions, in the nineteenth century—strange enough.

"And so," continued I aloud, "you have pilgrims at Clonmacnoise?"

"Troth we have, your honour, from the top of the north and the farthest corner of Kerry; and you may see them any day in the week, let alone the pathern (patron) day, when all the world, you'd think, was there."

"And the palace," said I, "I suppose belonged to the bishop of Clonmacnoise?"

"Some says 'twas the bishop, your honour, and indeed it is them that has larnin' says so: but more says 'twas a king had it long ago, afore the Churches was there at all at all; and sure enough it looks far oulder nor the churches, though them is ould enough God knows. All the knowledgable people I ever heerd talk of it, says that; and now, Sir," said he in an expostulatory tone, "wouldn't it be far more nath'ral that the bishop id live in the churches? And sure," continued he, evidently leaning to the popular belief, "id stands to *raison* that a king id live in a palace, and why *shud* it be called a palace if a king didn't live there?"

Satisfying himself with this most logical conclusion, he pulled his oar with evident self-complacency; and as I have always found, I derived more legendary information by yielding somewhat to the prejudice of the narrator, and by abstaining from inflicting any wound on his pride (so Irish a failing) by laughing at or endeavouring to combat his credulity, I seemed to favour his conclusions, and admitted that a king must have been the *ci-devant* occupant of the palace.

So much being settled, he proceeded to tell me that "there was a mighty *quare* story" about the last king that ruled Clonmacnoise; and having expressed an eager desire to hear the *quare story*—he seemed quite happy at being called on to fulfil the office of chronicler; and pulling his oar with an easier sweep, lest he might disturb the quiet hearing of his legend by the rude splash of the water, he prepared to tell his tale, and I, to devour up his discourse.

"Well, Sir, they say there was a king wanst lived in the palace beyant, and a sportin' fellow he was, and *Cead mile failte* [1] was the word in the palace; no one kem but was welkim and I go bail the sorra one left it without the deoch an' doris, [2]—well, to be sure, the king av coorse had the best of eatin' and drinkin', and there was bed and boord for the stranger, let alone the welkim for the neighbours—and a good neighbour he was by all accounts, until, as bad luck would have it, a crass ould bishop (the saints forgi' me for saying the word), kem to rule over the churches. Now, you must know, the king was a likely man, and, as I said already, he was a sportin' fellow, and by coorse a great favourite with the women; he had a smile and a wink for the crathers at every hand's turn, and the soft word, and the—the short and the long of it is, he was the *divil* among the girls.

"Well, Sir, it was all mighty well, untell the ould bishop I mintioned arrived at the Churches; but whin he kem, he tuk great scandal at the goings-an of the king, and he determined to cut him short in his coorses all at wanst; so with that whin the king wint to his duty, the bishop ups and he tells him that he must mend his manners, and all to that; and when the king said that the likes o' that was never tould him afore by the best priest o' them all, 'More shame for them that *wor* before me,' says the bishop.

"But to make a long story short, the king looked mighty black at the bishop, and the bishop looked twice blacker at him again, and so on, from bad to worse, till they parted the bittherest of inimies and the king that was the best o' friends to the churches afore, swore be this and be that, he'd vex them for it, and that he'd be even with the bishop afore long.

"Now, Sir, the bishop might jist as well have kept never mindin' the king's little *kimmeens* with the girls, for the story goes that he had a little failin' of his own in regard of a dhrop, and that he knew the differ betune wine and wather, for, poor ignorant crathurs, it's little they knew about whiskey in them days. Well, the king used often to send *lashins* o' wine to the Churches, by the way, as he said, that they should have plinty of it for celebrating the mass—although he knew well that it was a little of it went far that-a-way and that their Riverinces was fond of a hearty glass as well as himself, and why not, Sir?—if they'd let him alone; for, says the king, as many a one said afore, and will again, I'll make a child's bargain with you, says he, do you let me alone, and I'll let you alone; *manin'* by that, Sir, that if they'd ay nothin' about the girls, he would give them plinty of wine.

"And so it fell out a little before he had the *scrimmage*[3] with the bishop, the king promised them a fine store of wine that was comin' up the Shannon in boats, Sir, and big boats they wor, I'll go bail— not all as one as the little *drolleen* (wren) of a thing we're in now, but nigh-hand as big as a ship; and there was three of these fine boats- full comin'—two for himself, and one for the churches; and so says the king to himself 'the divil receave the dhrop of that wine they shall get,' says he, 'the dirty beggarly neygars; bad cess to the dhrop,' says he, 'my big-bellied bishop, to nourish your jolly red nose—I said I'd be even with you,' says he, 'and so I will; and if you spoil my divarshin, I'll spoil yours, and turn about is fair play, as the divil said to the smoke-jack.' So with that, Sir, the king goes and he gives ordhers to his sarvants how it wid be when the boats kem up the river with the wine—and more especial to one in partic'lar they called Corny, his own man, by raison he was mighty stout, and didn't love priests much more nor himself.

"Now Corny, Sir, let alone bein' stout, was mighty dark, and if he wanst said the word, you might as well sthrive to move the rock of Dunamaise as Corny, though without a big word at all at all, but as *quite* (quiet) as a child. Well, in good time, up kem the boats, and down runs the monks, all as one as a flock o' crows over a cornfield, to pick up whatever they could for themselves; but troth the king was afore them, for all his men was there, and Corny at their head.

"'*Dominus vobiscum,*' (which manes, God save you, Sir,) says one of the monks to Corny, 'we kem down to save you the throuble of unloading the wine, which the king, God bless him, gives to the church.'

"Oh, no throuble in life, plaze your Riverince,' says Corny, 'we'll unload it ourselves, your Riverince,' says he.

"So with that they began unloading, first one boat, and then another; but sure enough, every individual cashk of it went up to the palace, and not a one to the Churches: so whin they seen the second boat a'most empty; quare thoughts began to come into their heads, for before this offer, the first boatload was always sent to the bishop, afore a dhrop was taken to the king, which, you know, was good manners, Sir; and the king, by all accounts, was a gintleman, every inch of him. So, with that, says one of the monks:

"'My blessin' an you, Corny, my son,' says he, 'sure it's not forgettin' the bishop you'd be, nor the churches,' says he, 'that stands betune you and the divil.'

"Well, Sir, at the word divil, 'twas as good as a play to see the look Corny gave out o' the corner of his eye at the monk.

"'Forget yez,' says Corny, 'throth it's long afore me or my *masther,*' says he, (nodding his head a bit at the word,) 'will forget the bishop of Clonmacnoise. Go an with your work, boys,' says he to the men about him, and away they wint, and soon finished unloadin' the second boat; and with that they began at the third.

"'God bless your work, boys,' says the bishop; for, sure enough, 'twas the bishop himself kem down to the river side, having got the *hard word* of what was goin' an. 'God bless your work,' says he, as they heaved the first barrel of wine out of the boat. 'Go, help them, my sons,' says he, turning round to half a dozen strappin' young priests as was standing by.

"'No occasion in life, plaze your Riverince,' says Corny; 'I'm intirely obleeged to your lordship, but we're able for the work ourselves,' says he. And without sayin' another word, away went the barrels out of the boat, and up on their shoulders, or what ever way they wor takin' it, and up the hill to the palace.

"'Hillo!' says the bishop, 'where are yiz goin' with that wine?' says he.

"'Where I tould them,' says Corny.

"'Is it to the palace?' says his Riverince.

"'Faith, you jist hit it,' says Corny.

"'And what's that for?' says the bishop.

"'For fun,' says Corny, no ways *frikened* at all by the dark look the bishop gave him. And sure it's a wondher the fear of the church didn't keep him in dread—but Corny was the divil intirely.

"'Is that the answer you give your clargy, you reprobate?' says the bishop. 'I'll tell you what it is, Corny,' says he, 'as sure as your standin' there I'll excommunicate you, my fine fellow, if you don't keep a civil tongue in your head.'

"'Sure it wouldn't be worth your Riverince's while,' says Corny, 'to excommunicate the likes o' me,' says he, 'while there's the king my masther to the fore, for your holiness to play bell, book and candle-light with.'

"'Do you mane to say, you scruff o' the earth,' says the bishop, 'that your masther, the king, put you up to what you're doing?'

"'Divil a thing else I mane,' says Corny.

"'You *villian!*' says the Bishop, 'the king never did the like.'

"'Yes, but I did though,' says the king, puttin' in his word fair an aisy; for he was lookin' out o' his dhrawin'-room windy, and run down the hill to the river, when he seen the bishop goin', as he thought, to put his *comether* upon Corny.

"'So,' says the bishop, turnin' round quite short to the king—'so, my lord,' says he, 'am I to understand this villian has your commands for his purty behavor?'

"'He has my commands for what he done,' says the king, quite stout; 'and more be token, I'd have you to know he's no villian at all,' says he, 'but a thrusty sarvant, that does his masther's biddin'.'

"'And don't you intind sendin' any of this wine over to my churches beyant?' says the bishop.

"'The divil reserve the dhrop,' says the king.

"'And what for?' says the bishop.

"'Bekase I've changed my mind,' says the king.

"'And won't you give the church wine for the holy mass?' says the bishop.

"'The mass!' says the king, eyin' him mighty sly.

"'Yes, Sir—the mass,' says his Riverince, colouring up to the eyes—'the mass.'

"'Oh, *baithershin!*' says the king.

"'What do you mane?' says the bishop—and his nose got blue with fair rage.

"'Oh, nothin',' says the king, with a toss of his head.

"'Are you a gintleman?' says the bishop.

"'Every inch o' me,' says the king.

"'Then sure no gintleman goes back of his word,' says the other.

"'I wont go back o' my word, either,' says the king.—'I promised to give wine for the mass,' says he, 'and so I will. Send to my palace every Sunday mornin', and you shall have a bottle of wine, and that's plinty; for I'm thinkin',' says the king, 'that so much wine lyin' beyant there, is neither good for your bodies nor your sowls.'

"'What do you mane?' say the bishop in a great passion, for all the world like a turkey-cock.

"'I mane, that when your wine-cellar is so full,' says the king, 'it only brings the fairies about you, and makes away with the wine too fast,' says he, laughin'; 'and the fairies to be about the churches isn't good, your Riverince,' says the king; 'for I'm thinkin',' says he, 'that some of the spiteful little divils has given your Riverince a blast, and burnt the end of your nose.'

"With that, my dear, you couldn't hould the bishop, with the rage he was in; and says he, 'You think to dhrink all that wine—but you're mistaken,' says he—'fill your cellars as much as you like,' says the bishop, '*but you'll die iv drooth yit;*—and with that he went down on his knees and cursed the king (God betune us and harm!) and shakin' his fist at him, he gother [gathered] all his monks about him, and away they wint home to the churches.

"Well, Sir, sure enough, the king fell sick of a suddent, and all the docthors in the country round was sent for;—but they could do him no good at all at all—and day by day he was wastin' and wastin', and pinin' and pinin', till the flesh was worn off his bones, and he was as bare and as yellow as a kite's claw; and then, what would you think, but the drooth came an him sure enough, and he was caffin' for dhrink every *minit*, till you'd think he'd dhrink the *sae* dhry.

"Well, when the clock struck twelve that night, the drooth was an him worse nor ever, though he dhrunk as much that day—ay, troth, as much as would turn a mill; and he called to his servants for a dhrink of *grule* [gruel].

"'The grule's all out,' says they.

"'Well, then, give me some *whay,*' says he.

"'There's none left, my lord,' says they.

"'Then give me a dhrink of wine,' says he.

"'There's none in the room, dear,' says the nurse-tindher.

"'Then go down to the wine-cellar,' says he, 'and get some.'

"With that, they wint to the wine-cellar—but, jew'l machree, they soon run back into his room, with their faces as white as a sheet, and tould him there was not one dhrop of wine in all the cashks in the cellar.

"'Oh murther! murther!' says the king, '*I'm dyin' of drooth,*' says he.

"And then, God help iz! they bethought themselves of what the bishop said, and the curse he laid an the king.

"'You've no grule?' says the king.

"'No,' says they.

"'Nor *whay?*'

"'No,' says the sarvants.

"'Nor wine?' says the king.

"'Nor wine either, my lord,' says they.

"'Have you no *tay*?' says he.

"'Not a dhrop,' says the nurse-tindher.

"'Then,' says the king, 'for the tindher marcy of God, gi' me a dhrink of wather.'

"And what would you think, Sir, but there wasn't a dhrop of wather in the place.

"'Oh, murther! murther!' says the king, 'isn't it a poor case, that a king can't get a dhrink of wather in his own house? Go then,' says he, 'and get me a jug of wather out of the ditch.'

"For there was a big ditch, Sir, all round the palace. And away they run for wather out of the ditch, while the king was roarin' like mad for the drooth, and his mouth like a coal of fire. And sure, Sir, the story goes, they couldn't find any wather in the ditch!

"'Millia murther! millia murther!' cries the king, 'will no one take pity an a king that's *dyin' for the bare drooth?*'

"And they all thrimbled again, with the fair fright, when they heerd this, and thought of the ould bishop's prophecy.

"'Well,' says the poor king, 'run down to the Shannon,' says he, 'and sure, at all events, you'll get wather there,' says he.

"Well, Sir, away they run with pails and noggins, down to the Shannon, and (God betune us and harm!) what do you think, Sir, but the river Shannon was dhry! So, av coorse, when the king heerd the Shannon was gone dhry, it wint to his heart; and he thought o' the bishop's curse an him—and, givin' one murtherin' big *screech,* that split the walls of the palace, as may be seen to this day, he died, Sir—makin' the bishop's words good, that '*he would die of drooth yit!*'

"And now, Sir," says my historian, with a look of lurking humour in his dark grey eye, "isn't that mighty wondherful—*iv it's thrue?*"

1.   A hundred thousand welcomes.
2.   The parting cup.
3.   Evidently derived from the French *escrimer.*

An Essay on Fools

A fool, a fool!—I met a fool i' the forest.

AS YOU LIKE IT

A S SOME ALLUSION HAS BEEN made of the foregoing story to a fool, this, perhaps, is the fittest place to say something of fools in general. Be it understood, I only mean fools by profession; for, were amateur fools included, an essay on fools in general would be no trifling undertaking. And, further, I mean to limit myself within still more circumscribed bounds, by treating of the subject only as it regards that immediate part of his Majesty's dominions called Ireland.

In Ireland, the fool, or natural, or innocent, (for by all those names he goes,) as represented in the stories of the Irish peasantry, is very much the fool that Shakspeare occasionally embodies; and even in the present day, many a witticism and sarcasm, given birth to by these mendicant Touchstones, would be treasured in the memory of our *beau monde*, under the different heads of brilliant or biting, had they been uttered by a Bushe or a Plunket. I recollect a striking piece of imagery employed by one of the tribe, on his perceiving the approach of a certain steward, who, as a severe task-master, had made himself disliked amongst the peasantry employed on his master's estate. This man had acquired a nick-name (Irishmen, by the way, are celebrated for the application of *sobriquets*), which nick name

was "Danger;" and the fool, standing one day amidst a parcel of workmen, who were cutting turf, perceived this said steward crossing the bog towards them: "Ah, ah! by dad, you must work now, boys," said he, "here comes Danger. Bad luck to you, daddy Danger, you dirty blood-sucker, sure the earth's heavy with you." But suddenly stopping in his career of common-place abuse, he looked with an air of contemplative dislike towards the man, and deliberately said, "There you are, Danger! and may I never break bread, *if all the turf in the bog 'id warm me to you.*"

Such are the occasional bursts of figurative language uttered by our fools, who are generally mendicants; or perhaps it would be fitter to call them dependants, either on some particular family, or on the wealthy farmers of the district. But they have a great objection that such should be supposed to be the case, and are particularly jealous of their independence. An example of this was given me by a friend, who patronised one that was rather a favourite of the gentlemen in the neighbourhood, and a constant attendant at every fair within ten or fifteen miles, where he was sure to pick up a good deal of money from his gentlemen friends. Aware of this fact, Mr —— meeting Jimmy[1] one morning on the road, and knowing what errand he was bound on, asked him where he was going?

"I'm goin' to the fair, your honour."

"Why, what can *you* bring you there?"

"Oh, I've business there."

"What business—?"

"I'll tell you to-morrow."

"Ah! Jimmy," said the gentleman, "I see how it is—you're going to the fair to ask all the gentlemen for money."

"Indeed I'm not: I'm no beggar—Jimmy wouldn't be a beggar. Do you think I've nothin' else to do but beg?"

"Well, what else brings you to the fair?"

"Sure I'm goin' to sell a cow there," said Jimmy, quite delighted at fancying he had successfully baffled the troublesome inquiries of the Squire: and not willing to risk another question or answer, he uttered his deafening laugh, and pursued his road to the fair.

From the same source I heard that they are admirable couriers, which my friend very fairly accounted for, by attributing it to the small capability of comprehension in the constitution of their minds, which, rendering them unable to embrace more than one idea at a time, produces a singleness of purpose, that renders them valuable messengers. As an instance of this, he told me that a gentleman in his neighbourhood once sent a certain fool to the town of —— with a packet of great consequence and value, to his banker, with a direction to the bearer not to hand it to any person but Mr — himself, and not to return without seeing him.

It so happened Mr — had gone to Dublin that morning; and no assurances nor persuasion, on the part of that gentleman's confidential clerk, could induce the fool to hand him the parcel—thus observing strict obedience to the commands of his master. But he adhered still more literally to his commission; for when he was told Mr — had gone to Dublin, and that, therefore, he could not give him the packet, he said, "Oh, very well, Jimmy 'ill go back again;" but when he left the office, he took the road to Dublin, instead of homewards, having been bidden not to return without delivering it, and ran the distance to the capital, (about one hundred and forty miles,) in so short a time, that he arrived there but a few hours after the gentleman he followed, and never rested until he discovered where he was lodged, and delivered to him the parcel, in strict accordance with his instructions.

They are affectionate also. I have heard of a fool, who, when some favourite member of a family he was attached to died, went to the church-yard, and sat on the grave, and there wept bitterly, and watched night and day; nor could he be forced from the place, nor could the calls of hunger and thirst induce him to quit the spot for many days; and such was the intensity of grief on the part of the affectionate creature, that he died in three months afterwards.

But they can be revengeful too, and entertain a grudge with great tenacity. The following is a ridiculous instance of this:—A fool, who had been severely bitten by a gander, that was unusually courageous, watched an opportunity, when his enemy was absent, and getting amongst the rising family of the gander, he began to trample upon the goslings, and was caught in the fact of murdering them wholesale, by the enraged woman who had reared them.

"Ha! Jimmy, you villian, is it murtherin' my lovely goslins you are, you thief of the world? Bad scram to you, you thick-headed vagabone."

"Divil mend them, granny," shouted Jimmy, with a laugh of idiotic delight, as he leaped over a ditch, out of the reach of the hen-wife, who rushed upon him with a broom-stick, full of dire intent upon Jimmy's skull.

"Oh, you moroadin' thief!" cried the exasperated woman, shaking her uplifted broomstick at Jimmy in impotent rage; "wait till Maurice ketches you—that's all."

"Divil mend them, granny," shouted Jimmy—"ha! ha!—why did their daddy bite me?"

The peasantry believe a fool to be insensible to fear, from any ghostly visitation; and I heard of an instance where the experiment was made on one of these unhappy creatures, by dressing a strapping fellow in a sheet, and placing him in a situation to intercept "poor Jimmy" on his midnight path, and try the truth of this generally-received opinion, by endeavouring to intimidate him. When he had reached the appointed spot, a particularly lonely and narrow path, and so hemmed in by high banks on each side, as to render escape difficult, Mr Ghost suddenly reared his sheeted person, as Jimmy had half ascended a broken stile, and with all the usual terrific formulae of "Boo," "Fee-fa-fum," &c., &c., demanded who dared to cross that path? The answer, "I'm poor Jimmy," was given in his usual tone. "I'm Raw-head and Bloody-bones," roared the ghost. "Ho! ho! I often heerd o' you," said Jimmy. "Baw," cried the ghost, advancing— I'll kill you—I'll kill you—I'll kill you." "The divil a betther opinion I had iv you," said Jimmy. "Boo!" says Raw-head "I'll eat you—I'll eat you." "The divil do you good with me," says Jimmy. And so the ghost was at a nonplus, and Jimmy won the field.

I once heard of a joint-stock company having been established between a fool and a blind beggar-man, and for whom the fool acted in the capacity of guide. They had share and share alike in the begging concern, and got on tolerably well together, until one day the blind man had cause to suspect Jimmy's honour. It happened that, a mail-coach passing by, the blind man put forth all his begging graces to induce the "quality" to "extind their charity," and succeeded so well, that not only some copper, but a piece of silver was thrown by the way side. Jimmy, I'm sorry to say, allowed "the filthy lucre of gain" so far to predominate, that in picking up these gratuities, he appropriated the silver coin to his own particular pouch, and brought the half pence only for division to his blind friend; but the sense of hearing was so nice in the latter, that he detected the sound of the falling silver, and asked Jimmy to produce it. Jimmy denied the fact stoutly. "Oh, I heerd it fall," said the blind man. "Then you were betther off than poor Jimmy," said our hero; "for you *heerd* it, but poor Jimmy didn't see it." "Well, look for it," says the blind man. "Well, well, but you're cute, daddy," cried Jimmy; "you're right enough, I see it now;" and Jimmy affected to pick up the sixpence, and handed it to his companion.

"Now we'll go an to the Squire's," said the blind man, "and they'll give us somethin' to eat;" and he and his idiot companion were soon seated outside the kitchen-door of the Squire's house, waiting for their expected dish of broken meat and potatoes.

Presently Jimmy was summoned, and he stepped forward to receive the plate that was handed him; but in its transit from the kitchen-door to the spot where the blind man was seated, Jimmy played foul again, by laying violent hands on the meat, and leaving potatoes only in the dish. Again the acute sense of the blind man detected the fraud; he sniffed the scent of the purloined provision; and after poking with hurried fingers amongst the potatoes, he exclaimed, "Ha! Jimmy, Jimmy, I smelt meat." "Deed and deed, no," said Jimmy, who had, in the mean time, with the voracity of brutal hunger, devoured his stolen prey. "That's a lie, Jimmy," said the blind man—"that's like the sixpence. Ha! you thievin' rogue, to cheat a poor blind man, you villian;" and forthwith he aimed a blow of his stick at Jimmy with such good success, as to make the fool bellow lustily. Matters, however, were accommodated; and both parties considered that the beef and the blow pretty well balanced one another, and so accounts were squared.

After their meal at the Squire's, they proceeded to an adjoining villa; but in the course of their way thither, it was necessary to pass a rapid, and sometimes swollen, mountain-stream, and the only means of transit was by large blocks of granite placed at such intervals in the stream, as to enable a passenger to step from one to the other, and hence called "stepping-stones." Here, then, it was necessary, on the blind man's part, to employ great caution, and he gave himself up to the guidance of Jimmy, to effect his purpose. "You'll tell me where I'm to step," said he, as he cautiously approached the brink. "Oh, I will, daddy," said Jimmy; "give me your hand."

But Jimmy thought a good opportunity had arrived, for disposing of one whom he found to be an over-intelligent companion, and leading him to a part of the bank where no friendly stepping-stone was placed, he cried, "step out now, daddy." The poor blind man obeyed the command, and tumbled plump into the water. The fool screamed with delight, and clapped his hands. The poor deluded blind man floundered for some time in the stream, which, fortunately, was not sufficiently deep to be dangerous; and when he scrambled to the shore, he laid about him with his stick and tongue, in dealing blows and anathemas, all intended for Jimmy. The former Jimmy carefully avoided, by running out of the enraged blind man's reach. "Oh, my curse light an you, you black-hearted thraitor," said the dripping old beggar, "that has just wit enough to be wicked, and to play such a hard-hearted turn to a poor blind man." "Ha! ha! daddy," cried Jimmy, "*you could smell the mate—why didn't you smell the wather?*"

1.　This is the name almost universally applied here to fools. *Tom* seems to be the one in use in England, even as far back as Shakspeare's time: but Jimmy is the established name in Ireland.

THE CATASTROPHE

> I was by at the opening of the fardel.
> Methought I heard the shepherd say he found a child.

JOHN DAW, OF THE COUNTY ——, gent., who, from his propensity to look down his neighbours' chimneys, was familiarly called Mr Jackdaw, was a man, who (to adopt a figure of speech which he often used himself), could see as far into a millstone as most people. He could play at politics, as boys play at marbles—and Mr Daw could be down upon any king's taw, as best suited his pleasure, and prove he was quite right, to boot, provided you would only listen to his arguments, and not answer them. Though to say the truth, Mr Daw seldom meddled with so august a personage as a king—he was rather of Shakspeare's opinion, that

> There's a divinity doth hedge a king;

and after the fall of Napoleon, whom he could abuse to his heart's content, with all the hackneyed epithets of tyrant, monster, &c., without any offence to legitimacy, his rage against royalty was somewhat curtailed of its "fair proportions." But still, politics always afforded him a very pretty allowance of hot water to dabble in. Of course, he who could settle the affairs of nations with so much satisfaction to himself, could also superintend those of his neighbours;

and the whole county, if it knew but all, had weighty obligations to Mr Daw, for the consideration he bestowed on the concerns of every man in it, rather than his own. But the world is very ill-natured, and the county —— in particular; for while Mr Daw thus exhibited so much interest in the affairs of his acquaintances, they only called him "bore—busy-body—meddler," and other such-like amiable appellations.

No stolen "march of intellect" had ever been allowed to surprise the orthodox outposts of Mr Daw's understanding. He was for the good old times—none of your heathenish innovations for him! The word liberality was an abomination in his ears, and strongly reminded him of "Popery, slavery, arbitrary power, brass money and wooden shoes."

Two things he hated in particular—cold water and papists—he thought them both bad for "the constitution." Now, the former of the aforesaid, Mr Daw took special good care should never make any innovation on his—and the bitterest regret of his life, was, that he had it not equally in his power to prevent the latter from making inroads upon that of the nation.

A severe trial of Mr Daw's temper existed, in the situation which a certain Roman Catholic chapel held, on the road which led from his house to the parochial Protestant church. This chapel was a singularly humble little building, whose decayed roof of straw gave evidence of the poverty and inability of the flock who crowded within it every Sunday, to maintain a more seemly edifice for the worship of God. It was situated immediately on the roadside, and so inadequate was it in size to contain the congregation which flocked to it for admittance, that hundreds of poor people might be seen every Sabbath, kneeling outside the door, and stretching in a crowd so dense across the road, as to occasion considerable obstruction to a passenger thereon. This was always a source of serious annoyance to the worthy Mr Daw; and one Sunday in particular, so great was the concourse of people, that he was absolutely obliged to stop his jaunting-car, and was delayed the enormous space of a full minute and a half, before the offending worshippers could get out of the way. This was the climax of annoyance—it was insufferable. That he should have, every Sunday as he went to church, his Christian serenity disturbed by passing so heathenish a temple as a mass-house, and witness the adoration of "damnable idolaters," was bad enough; but that he, one of the staunchest Protestants in the county, one of the most unflinching of the sons of ascendancy, should be delayed upon his way to church by a pact of "rascally rebelly papists," as he charitably called them, was beyond endurance, and he deeply swore he would never go to church by that road again, to be obnoxious to so great an indignity. And he kept his word. He preferred going a round of five miles to the ample and empty church of ——, than again pass the confined and crowded little chapel.

This was rather inconvenient sometimes, to be sure, when autumn rains and winter snows were falling—but no matter. The scene of his degradation was not to be passed for any consideration, and many a thorough drenching and frost-bitten penalty were endured in the cause of ascendancy; but what then?—he had the reward in his own breast, and he bore all with the fortitude of a martyr, consoling himself in the notion of his being a "suffering loyalist."

If he went out of his way to avoid one popish nuisance, he was "*put* out of his way" by another—namely, by having his residence in the vicinity of a convent. Yea, within ear-shot of their vesper music lay his pleasure-ground; and a stone wall (a very strong and high one, to be sure) was all that interposed itself between his Protestant park and the convent garden.

Both of these lay upon the shore of the expansive Shannon; and "a time and oft," when our hero was indulging in an evening stroll on the bank of the river, did he wish the poor nuns fairly at the bottom of it, as their neighbouring voices, raised perchance in some hymn to the Virgin, smote the tympanum of his offended ear.

He considered, at length, that this proximity to a convent, which at first he deemed such an hardship, might be turned to account, in a way, of all others, congenial to his disposition, by affording him an opportunity of watching the movements of its inmates. Of the nefarious proceedings of such a body—of their numberless intrigues,

&c., &c., he himself had no doubt, and he forthwith commenced a system of *espionage,* that he might be enabled to produce proof for the conviction of others. During the day, there was a provoking propriety preserved about the place, that excited Mr Daw's wrath— "ay, ay," would he mutter to himself, "they were always deep as well as dangerous—they're too cunning to commit themselves by any thing that might be easily discovered; but wait—wait until the moonlight nights are past, and I warrant my watching shan't go for nothing."

Under the dewy damps of night, many an hour did Mr Daw hold his *surveillance* around the convent bounds; but still fortune favoured him not in this enterprise; and not one of the delinquencies which he had no doubt were going forward, had he the good fortune to discover. No scarf was waved from the proscribed casements—no ladder of ropes was to be found attached to the forbidden wall—no boat, with muffled oar, stealthily skimming along the waters, could be detected in the act of depositing "a gallant gay Lothario" in the Hesperian garden, where, he doubted not, many an adventurous Jason plucked forbidden fruit.

Chance, however, threw in his way a discovery, which all his premeditated endeavours had formerly failed to accomplish; for one evening, just as the last glimmer of departing day was streaking the west, Mr Daw, in company with a friend (a congenial soul), when returning after a long day's shooting, in gleeful anticipation of a good dinner, heard a sudden splash in the water, apparently proceeding from the extremity of the convent-wall, to which point they both directly hurried. What the noise originated in, we shall soon see; but a moment's pause must be first given to say a word or two of Mr Daw's friend.

He was a little bustling man, always fussing about something or other—eternally making frivolous excuses for paying visits at unseasonable hours, for the purpose of taking people by surprise, and seeing what they were about, and everlastingly giving people advice; and after any unpleasant accident, loss of property, or other casualty, he was always ready with an assurance, that "if that had been his case, he would have done so and so;" and gave ample grounds for you to understand that you were very little more or less than a fool, and he the wisest of men since the days of Solomon.

But curiosity was his prevailing foible. When he entered a room, his little twinkling eyes went peering round the chamber, to ascertain if any thing worth notice was within eye-shot; and when failure ensued, in that case he himself went on a voyage of discovery into ever corner, and with excuses so plausible, that he flattered himself nobody saw what he did. For example, he might commence thus—"Ha! Miss Emily, you've got a string broken in your harp, I see,"—forthwith he posted over to the instrument; and while he was clawing the strings and declaring it was "a monstrous sweet harp," he was reconnoitring the quarter where it stood, with the eye of a lynx. Unsuccessful there, he would proceed, mayhap, to the table, where some recently received letters were lying, and stooping down over one with its seal upwards, exclaim, "Dear me! what a charming device! Let me see—what is it?—a padlock, and the motto 'honour keeps the key.' Ah! very pretty indeed—excellent." And then he would carelessly turn over the letter, to see the post-mark and superscription, to try if he could glean any little *hint* from them—"So, so! a foreign post-mark. I see—ha! I dare say, now, this is from your cousin—his regiment's abroad, I believe? Eh! Miss Emily?" (rather knowingly). Miss Emily might reply slyly, "I thought you admired the *motto* on the seal?" "Oh, yes—a—very true, indeed—a very pretty motto;"—and so on.

This little gentleman was, moreover, very particular in his dress; the newest fashions were sure to be exhibited on his diminutive person; and from the combined quality of *petit maître* and eavesdropper, he enjoyed a *sobriquet* as honourable as Mr Daw, and was called *Little Beau Peep.*

Upon one occasion, however, while minding his neighbours' affairs with an exemplary vigilance, some sheep-stealers made free with a few of his flock, and though so pre-eminently prompt in the suggestion of preventions or remedies in similar cases, when his friends were in trouble, he could not make the slight movement towards the recovery of his own property. All his *dear friends* were, of course, delighted; and so far did they carry their exultation in his mishap, that some one, a night or two after his disaster, pasted on his hall door the following quotation from a celebrated nursery ballad;—

> Little Beau Peep
> Has lost his sheep,
> And does not know where to find them.

He had a little dog, too, that was as great a nuisance as himself, and emulated his master in his prying propensities; he was very significantly called "Ferret," and not unfrequently had he been instrumental in making mischievous discoveries. One in particular I cannot resist noticing:—

Mrs Fitz-Altamont was a lady of high descent—in short, the descent had been such a long one, that the noble family of Fitz-Altamont had descended very low indeed—but Mrs Fitz-Altamont would never let "the aspiring blood of Lancaster sink in the ground;" and, accordingly, was always reminding her acquaintances how very noble a stock she came from, at the very moment, perhaps, she was making some miserable show of gentility. In fact, Mrs Fitz-Altamont's mode of living reminded one very much of worn-out plated ware, in which the copper makes a very considerable appearance; or, as Goldsmith says of the French, she

> Trimm'd her robe of frieze with copper lace.

Her children had been reared from their earliest infancy with lofty notions; they started, even from the baptismal font, under the shadow of high-sounding names; there were Alfred, Adolphus, and Harold, her magnanimous boys, and Angelina and Iphigenia, her romantic girls.

Judge then of the mortification of Mrs Fitz-Altamont, when one day, seated at rather a homely early dinner, Little Beau Peep popped in upon them.—How he contrived such a surprise is not stated—whether by a surreptitious entry through a back window, or, fairy-like, through a key-hole, has never been clearly ascertained—but certain it is, he detected the noble family of Fitz-Altamont in the fact of having been dining upon—EGGS!—yes, sympathetic reader—EGGS!—The *denouement* took place thus:—Seated before this unseemly fare, the noise of Beau Peep was heard in the hall by the affrighted Fitz-Altamonts. No herd of startled deer was ever half so terrified by the deep bay of the ferocious stag-hound, as "the present company" at the shrill pipe of the cur, Beau Peep; and by a simultaneous movement of thought and action they at once huddled every thing upon the table, topsy turvy, into the table cloth, and crammed it with precipitous speed under the sofa; and scattering the chairs from their formal and indicative position round the table, they met their "*dear friend*" Beau Peep with smiles, as he gently opened the door in his own insinuating manner, to say, that "just as he was in the neighbourhood, he would not pass by his esteemed friend, Mrs Fitz-Altamont, without calling to pay his respects." Both parties were "*delighted*" to see each other, and Mr Beau Peep seated himself on the sofa, and his little dog "Ferret" lay down between his feet; and whether it was from a spice of his master's talent for discovery, or a keen nose that nature gave him, we know not—but after sniffing once or twice, he made a sudden dart beneath the sofa, and in an instant emerged from under its deep and dirty flounce, dragging after him the table-cloth, which, unfolding in its course along the well-darned carpet, disclosed "a beggarly account of empty" egg-shells.

We shall not attempt to describe the *finale* of such a scene; but Mrs Fitz-Altamont, in speaking to a friend on the subject, when the affair had "got wind," and demanded an explanation, declared she never was so "horrified" in her life. It was just owing to her own foolish good-nature; she had allowed all her servants (she had *one*) to go to the fair in the neighbourhood, and had ordered John to be at home at a certain hour from the town, with marketing. But John did not return; and it happened so unfortunately—such a thing never happened before in her house—there was not an atom in the larder but eggs, and they just were making a little *lunch,* when that provoking creature, Mr Terrier, broke in on them.

"My dear Madam, if you had only seen it: Alfred *had* eaten his egg—Adolphus *was* eating his egg—Harold was in the act of *cracking* his egg—and I was just putting some salt in my egg, (indeed I spilt the salt a moment before, and was certain something un-lucky was going to happen)—and the dear romantic girls, Angelina and Iphigenia, were at the moment boiling their eggs, when that dreadful little man got into the house. It's very laughable, to be sure—he! he! he!—when one knows all about it; but *really* I was never so provoked in my life."

We ask pardon for so long a digression; but an anxiety to show what sort of person Little Beau Peep was, has betrayed us into it; and we shall now hurry to the developement of our story.

We left Beau Peep and Jack Daw hurrying off towards the convent-wall, where it was washed by the river, to ascertain what caused the loud splash in the water, which they heard, and has already been noticed. On arriving at the extremity of Mr Daw's grounds, they perceived the stream yet agitated, apparently from the sudden immersion of something into it; and, on looking more sharply through the dusk, they saw, floating rapidly down the current, a basket, at some distance, but not so far away as to prevent their hearing a faint cry, evidently proceeding from it; and the next moment they heard a female voice say, in the adjoining garden of the convent, "There let it go; the nasty creatures, to do such a horrid thing—"

"Did. you hear that?" said Mr Daw.

"I did," said Beau Peep.

"There's proof positive," said Daw. "The villainous papist jades, one of them has had a child, and some of her dear sisters are drowning it for her, to conceal her infamy."

"No doubt of it," said Beau Peep.

"I knew it all along," said Jack Daw. "Come, my dear friend," added he, "let us hasten back to O'Brien's cottage, and he'll row us down the river in his boat, and we may yet be enabled to reach the basket in time to possess ourselves of the proof of all this popish profligacy."

And off they ran to O'Brien's cottage; and hurrying O'Brien and his son to unmoor their boats, in which the gentleman had passed a considerable part of the day sporting, they jumped into the skiff, and urged the two men to pull away as fast as they could after the prize they hoped to obtain. Thus, hungry, and anxious for the dinner that was awaiting them all the time, their appetite for scandal was so much more intense, that they relinquished the former in pursuit of the latter.

"An' where is it your honour's goin'?" demanded O'Brien.

"Oh, a little bit down the river here," answered Mr Daw; for he did not wish to let it be known what he was in quest of, or his suspicions touching it, lest the peasants might baffle his endeavours at discovery, as he was sure they would strive to do in such a case, for the honour of the creed to which they belonged.

"Throth then, it's late your honour's agoin' an the wather this time o' day, and the night comin' an."

"Well, never mind that you, but pull away."

"By my sowl, I'll pull like a young cowlt, if that be all, and Jim too, Sir (that's your sort, Jimmy); but at this gate o' goin', the sorra far off the rapids will be long, and sure if we go down them now, the dickens a back we'll get to-night."

"O, never mind that," said Daw, "we can return by the fields."

As O'Brien calculated, they soon reached the rapids, and he called out to Jim to "studdy the boat there;" and with skilful management the turbulent descent was passed in safety, and they glided onwards again, under the influence of their oars, over the level waters.

"Do you see it yet?" asked one of the friends to the other, who replied in the negative.

"Maybe it's the deep hole your honour id be lookin' for?" queried O'Brien, in that peculiar vein of inquisitiveness which the Irish peasant indulges in, and through which he hopes, by pre-supposing a motive of action, to discover in reality the object aimed at.

"No," answered Daw, rather abruptly.

"Oh, it's only bekase it's a choice place of settin' night-lines," said O'Brien; "and I was thinkin' maybe it's for that your honour id be."

"Oh!" said Beau Peep, "'tis nothing more than is caught by night-lines we're seeking—eh, Daw?"

"Aye, aye, and, by Jove, I think I see it a little way before us—pull, O'Brien, pull!" and the boat trembled under the vigorous strokes of O'Brien and his son, and in a few minutes they were within an oar's length of the basket, which, by this time, was nearly sinking, and a moment or two later had deprived Jack Daw and Beau Peep of the honour of the discovery which they were now on the eve of completing.

"Lay hold of it," said Mr Daw; and Beau Peep, in "making a long arm," to secure the prize, so far overbalanced himself, that he went plump, head foremost, into the river; and had it not been for the activity and strength of the elder O'Brien, this our pleasant history must have turned out a tragedy of the darkest dye, and many a subsequent discovery of the indefatigable Beau Peep have remained in the unexplored depths of uncertainty. But, fortunately for the lovers of family secrets, the inestimable Beau Peep was drawn, dripping, from the river, by O'Brien, at the same moment that Jack Daw, with the boat-hook, secured the basket.

"I've got it!" exclaimed Daw, in triumph.

"Ay, and *I've got it, too*," chattered forth poor Beau Peep.

"'What's the matter with you, my dear friend?" said Daw, who in his anxiety to obtain the basket never perceived the fatality that had befallen his friend.

"I've been nearly drowned, that's all," whined forth the unhappy little animal, as he was shaking the water out of his ears.

"Throth, it was looky I had my hand so ready," said O'Brien, "or faith, maybe it's more nor a basket we'd have to be lookin' for."

"My dear fellow," said Daw, "let us get ashore immediately, and, by the exercise of walking, you may counteract the bad effects that this accident might otherwise produce. Get the boat ashore, O'Brien, as fast as possible. But we have got the basket, however, and that's some consolation for you."

"Yes," said the shivering little scandal-hunter, "I don't mind the drenching, since we have secured that."

"Why thin," as he pulled towards the shore, "may I make so bowld as to ax your honour, what curiosity there is in an owld basket, to make yiz take so much throuble and nigh hand drowndin' yourselves afore you cotcht it?"

"Oh, never you mind," said Mr Daw; "you shall soon know all about it. By-the-bye, my dear friend," turning to Terrier, "I think we had better proceed, as soon as we get ashore, to our neighbour Sturdy's—his is the nearest house we know of; there you may be enabled to change your wet clothes, and he being a magistrate, we can swear our informations against the delinquents in this case."

"Very true," said the unfortunate Beau Peep, as he stepped ashore, assisted by O'Brien, who, when the gentlemen proceeded some paces in advance, said to his son who bore the dearly-won basket, that "the poor little whelp (meaning Beau Peep) looked for all the world like a dog in a wet sack."

On they pushed, at a smart pace, until the twinkling of lights through some neighbouring trees announced to them the vicinity of Squire Sturdy's mansion. The worthy Squire had just taken his first glass of wine after the cloth had been drawn, when the servant announced the arrival of Mr Daw, and his half-drowned friend, who were at once ushered into the dining-room.

"Good heavens!" exclaimed the excellent lady of the mansion (for the ladies had not yet withdrawn), on perceiving the miserable plight of Beau Peep, "what has happened?"

"Indeed, madam," answered our little hero, "an unfortunate accident on the water—"

"Oh, ho!" said the Squire; "I should think that quite in your line—just exploring the secrets of the river? Why, my dear Sir, if you go on at this rate, making discoveries by water, as well as by land, you'll rival Columbus himself before long." And Miss Emily, of whom we have already spoken, whispered her mamma, that she had often heard of a diving-bell (*belle*), but never before of a diving *beau*.

"Had you not better change your clothes?" said Mrs Sturdy, to the shivering Terrier.

"Thank you, madam," said he, somewhat loftily, being piqued at the manner of his reception by the Squire, "I shall wait till an investigation has taken place, in my presence, of a circumstance which I have contributed to bring to light; and my discoveries by water may be found to be not undeserving of notice."

"I assure you, Mr Sturdy," added Mr Daw, in his most impressive manner, "we have an information to swear to, before you, of the most vital importance, and betraying the profligacy of certain people in so flagrant a degree, that I hope it may, at length, open the eyes of those that are wilfully blind to the interests of their king and their country."

This fine speech was meant as a hit at Squire Sturdy, who was a blunt, honest man—who acted in most cases, to the best of his ability, on the admirable Christian maxim of loving his neighbour as himself.

"Well, Mr Daw," said the Squire, "I am all attention to hear your information—"

"May I trouble you," said Daw, "to retire to your study, as the matter is rather of an indelicate nature, and not fit for ladies' ears?"

"No, no. We'll stay here, and Mrs S. and my daughters will retire to the drawing room. Go, girls, and get the tea ready;" and the room was soon cleared of the ladies, and the two O'Briens were summoned to wait upon the Squire in the dining room, with the important basket.

When they entered, Mr Daw, with a face of additional length and solemnity, unfolded to Squire Sturdy how the attention of his friend and himself had been attracted by a basket flung from the convent garden—how they ran to the spot—how they heard a faint cry; "and then, Sir," said he, "we were at once awake to the revolting certainty, that the nuns had thus intended secretly to destroy one of their own illegitimate offspring."

"Cross o' Christ about us!" involuntarily muttered forth the two O'Briens, making the sign of the cross at the same time on their foreheads.

"But have you any proof of this?" asked the magistrate.

"Yes, Sir," said Beau Peep, triumphantly, "we have proof—proof positive! Bring forward that basket," said he to the boatman. "There, Sir, is the very basket containing the evidence of their double guilt—first, the guilt of unchastity, and next, the guilt of infanticide; and it was in laying hold of that basket, that I met the accident, Mr Sturdy, that has occasioned you so much mirth. However, I believe you will acknowledge now, Mr Sturdy, that my discoveries by water have been rather important—?"

Here Mr Daw broke in, by saying, that the two boatmen were witnesses to the fact of finding the basket.

"Oh! by this and that," roared out O'Brien, "the devil resave the bit of a child I seen, I'll be upon my oath! and I wouldn't say that in a lie—"

"Be silent, O'Brien," said the magistrate. "Answer me, Mr Daw, if you please, one or two questions:—

"Did one or both of you see the basket thrown from the convent garden?"

"Both of us."

"And you heard a faint cry from it?"

"Yes—we heard the cry of an infant."

"You then rowed after the basket, in O'Brien's boat?"

"Is this the basket you saw the gentleman pick up, O'Brien?"

"Yes."

"By my sowl, I can't exactly say, your honor, for I was picking up Mr Terrier."

"It was you, then, that saved Mr Terrier from drowning?"

"Yes, Sir, undher God—"

"Fortunate that O'Brien was so active, Mr Terrier. Well, O'Brien, but that is the same basket you have carried here from the river?"

"Troth I don't know where I could change it an the road, Sir—"

"Well, let us open the basket, and see what it contains:"—and O'Brien commenced unlacing the cords that bound up the wicker-tomb of the murdered child; but so anxious was Mr Daw for prompt product of his evidence, that he took out his pen-knife, and cut the fastenings.

"Now; take it out," said Mr Daw; and every eye was riveted on the basket, as O'Brien, lifting the cover, and putting in his hand, said,

"Oh, then, but it's a beautiful baby!"—and he turned up a look of the tenderest pity at the three gentlemen.

"Pull it out here!" said Mr Daw, imperatively; and O'Brien, with the utmost gentleness, lifting the lifeless body from the basket, produced—A DROWNED CAT!

"O then, isn' it a darlint?" said O'Brien, with the most provoking affectation of pathos in his voice, while sarcasm was playing on his lip, and humour gleaming from his eye, as he witnessed with enjoyment the vacant stare of the discomfited Daw and Beau Peep, and exchanged looks with the worthy Squire, who had set up a horse-laugh the instant that poor pussy had made her appearance; and the moment he could recover his breath, exclaimed, "Why, by the L—d, it's a dead cat!"—and here upon the sound of smothered laughter reached them from outside the half-closed door, where the ladies, dear creatures! had stolen to listen, having been told that something not proper to hear was going forward.

The two grand inquisitors were so utterly confounded, that neither had a word to say; and as soon as the Squire had recovered from his immoderate fit of laughing, he said—"Well, gentlemen, this is a most important discovery you have achieved! I think I must despatch an express to government, on the strength of it."

"Oh, wait a bit, your honour," said O'Brien, "there's more o' hem yit;" and he took from out of the basket a handful of dead kittens.

Now, it happened that the cat had kittened in the convent that day, and, as it not unfrequently happens, the ferocious animal had destroyed some of her offspring, which so disgusted the nuns, that they bundled cat and kittens into an old basket, and threw them all into the river; and thus the "faint cry," and the words of the sisters, "the nasty creature, to do such a horrid thing," are at once explained.

"Why, this is worse than you anticipated, gentlemen," said the Squire, laughing—"for here, not only one, but several lives have been sacrificed."

"Mr Sturdy," said Mr Daw, very solemnly, "let me tell you, that if—"

"Tut! tut! my dear Sir," said the good-humoured Squire, interrupting him, "the wisest in the world may be deceived now and then; and no wonder your sympathies should have been awakened by the piercing cries of the helpless little sufferers."

"Throth, the sign's an it," said O'Brien; "it's aisy to see that the gentlemin has no childher of their own, for if they had, by my sowl, it's long before they'd mistake the cry of a dirty cat for a Christian child."

This was a bitter hit of O'Brien's, for neither Mrs Daw nor Mrs Terrier had ever been "as ladies wish to be who love their lords."

"I think," said the Squire, "we may now dismiss this affair; and after you have changed your clothes, Mr Terrier, a good glass of wine will do you no harm, for I see no use of letting the decanters lie idle any longer, since this *mysterious* affair has been elucidated."

"Throth, then, myself was thinking it a quare thing all along; for though sometimes a girl comes before your worship to sware a child agin a man, by the powers, I never heerd av a gintleman comin' to sware a child agin a woman yit—"

"Come, gentlemen," said the Squire, "the wine waits for us, and O'Brien and his son shall each have a glass of whiskey, to drink repose to the souls of the cats."

"Good luck to your honour," said O'Brien, "and the Misthress too—ah, by dad, it's *she* that knows the differ betune a cat and a child; and more power to your honour's elbow—"

But no entreaties on the part of Squire Sturdy could induce the discomfited Daw and Terrier to accept the Squire's proffered hospitality. The truth was, they were both utterly crest-fallen, and, as the ladies had overheard the whole affair, they were both anxious to get out of the house as fast as they could; so the Squire bowed them out of the hall-door—they wishing him a very civil good-night, and apologising for the trouble they had given him.

"Oh, don't mention it," said the laughing Squire, "really I have been very much amused; for of all the strange cases that have ever come within my knowledge, I have never met with so very curious a *cat*-astrophe!"

THE DEVIL'S MILL

His word is more than the miraculous harp;
He hath raised the wall, and houses too.

THE TEMPEST

BESIDE THE RIVER LIFFEY STANDS the picturesque ruins of a mill, overshadowed by some noble trees, that grow in great luxuriance at the water's edge. Here, one day, I was accosted by a silver-haired old man, that for some time had been observing me, and who, when I was about to leave the spot, approached me, and said, "I suppose it's after takin' off the ould mill you'd be, Sir?"

I answered in the affirmative.

"Maybe your honor id let me get a sight iv it," said he.

"With pleasure," said I, as I untied the strings of my portfolio, and, drawing the sketch from amongst its companions, presented it to him. He considered it attentively for some time, and at length exclaimed,

"Throth, there it is to the life—the broken roof and the wather-coorse; ay, even to the very spot where the gudgeon of the wheel was wanst, let alone the big stone at the corner, that was laid the first by *himself*;" and he gave the last word with mysterious emphasis, and handed the drawing back to me, with a "thankee, Sir," of most respectful acknowledgment.

"And who was 'himself,'" said I, "that laid that stone?" feigning ignorance, and desiring "to draw him out," as the phrase is.

"Oh, then, maybe it's what you'd be a stranger here?" said he.

"Almost," said I.

"And did you never hear tell of L——'s mill," said he, "and how it was built?"

"Never," was my answer.

"Throth then I thought young and ould, rich and poor, knew that—far and near."

"I don't, for one," said I; "but perhaps," I added, bringing forth some little preparation for a lunch, that I had about me, and producing a small flask of whiskey—"perhaps you will be so good as to tell me, and take a slice of ham, and drink my health," offering him a dram from my flask, and seating myself on the sod beside the river.

"Thank you kindly, Sir," says he; and so, after "warming his heart," as he said himself, he proceeded to give an account of the mill in question.

"You see, Sir, there was a man wanst, in times back, that owned a power of land about here—but God keep us, they said he didn't come by it honestly, but did a crooked turn whenever 'twas to sarve himself—and sure he *sowld the pass*,[1] and what luck or grace could he have afther that?"

"How do you mean he sold the pass?" said I.

"Oh, sure your honour must have heerd how the pass was sowld, and he bethrayed his king and counthry."

"No, indeed," said I.

"Och, well," answered my old informant, with a shake of the head, like Lord Burleigh in the *Critic*, to be very significant, "it's no matther now, and I don't care talkin' about it; and laist said is soonest mended—howsomever, he got a power of money for that same, and lands and what not; but the more he got, the more he craved, and there was no ind to his sthrivin' for goold evermore, and thirstin' for the lucre of gain.

"Well, at last, the story goes, the Divil (God bless us) kem to him, and promised him hapes o' money, and all his heart could desire, and more too, if he'd sell his soul in exchange."

"Surely he did not consent to such a dreadful bargain as that?" said I.

"Oh, no, Sir," said the old man, with a slight play of muscle about the corners of his mouth, which, but that the awfulness of the subject suppressed it, would have amounted to a bitter smile—"Oh no, he was too cunnin' for that, bad as he was—and he was bad enough, God knows—he had some regard for his poor sinful sowl, and he would not give himself up to the Divil, all out; but, the villian, he thought he might make a bargain with the *ould chap*, and get all he wanted, and keep himself out of harm's way still: for he was mighty 'cute—and throth he was able for ould Nick any day.

"Well, the bargain was struck: and it was this-a-way:—The Divil was to give him all the goold ever he'd ask for, and was to let him alone as long as he could; and the timpter promised him a long day, and said 'twould be a great while before he'd want him at all at all; and whin that time kem, he was to keep his hands aff him, as long as the other could give him some work he couldn't do.

"So, when the bargain was made, 'Now,' says the Colonel to the Divil, 'give me all the money I want.'

"'As much as you like,' says Ould Nick—'how much will you have?'

"'You must fill me that room,' says he, pointin' into a murtherin' big room, that he emptied out on purpose—'you must fill me that room,' says he, 'up to the very ceilin' with goolden guineas.'

"'And welkim,' says the Divil.

"With that, Sir, he began to shovel in the guineas into the room, like mad; and the Colonel towld him, that as soon as he was done, to come to him in his own parlour below, and that he would then go up and see if the Divil was as good as his word, and had filled the room with the goolden guineas. So the Colonel went down stairs, and the Ould Fellow worked away as busy as a nailer, shovellin' in the guineas by hundherds and thousands.

"Well, he worked away for an hour, and more, and at last he began to get tired; and he thought it *mighty odd* that the room wasn't fillin' fasther.—Well, afther restin' for a while, he began agin, and he put his shouldher to the work in airnest; but still the room was no fuller, at all at all.

"'Och! bad luck to me,' says the Divil, 'but the likes of this I never seen,' says he, 'far and near, up and down—the dickens a room I ever kem across afore,' says he, 'I couldn't cram while a cook would be crammin' a turkey, till now; and here I am,' says he, 'losin' my whole day, and I with such a power o' work an my hands yit, and this room no fuller than if I began five minutes ago.'

"By gor, while he was spakin', he seen the hape o' guineas in the middle of the flure growing *littler and littler* every minit; and at last they wor disappearing, for all the world, like corn in the hopper of a mill.

'Ho! ho!' says Ould Nick, 'is that the way wid you,' says he; and with that, he run over to the hape of goold—and what would you think, but it was runnin' down through a great big hole in the flure, that the Colonel made through the ceilin' in the room below; and that was the work he was at afther he left the Divil, though he purtended he was only waitin' for him in his parlour; and there the Divil, when he looked down through the hole in the flure, seen the Colonel, not content with the *two* rooms full of guineas, but with a big shovel, throwin' them into a closet a one side of him, as fast as they fell down. So, putting his head through the hole, he called down to the Colonel—'Hillo! neighbour,' says he.

"The Colonel look up, and grew as white as a sheet, when he seen he was found out, and the red eyes starin' down at him through the hole.

"'Musha, bad luck to your impudence!' says Ould Nick: 'is it sthriven to chate *me* you are,' says he, 'you villain?'

"'Oh! forgive me this wanst,' says the Colonel, 'and, upon the honour of a gintleman,' says he, 'I'll never—'

"'Whist! whisht! you thievin' rogue,' says the Divil—'I'm not angry with you, at all at all; but only like you the betther, bekase you're so cute—lave off slaving yourself there,' says he, 'you have got goold enough for this time; and whenever you want more, you have only to say the word, and it shall be yours at command.'

"So, with that, the Divil and he parted for that time: and myself doesn't know whether they used to meet often afther, or not; but the Colonel never wanted money, any how, but went on prosperous in the world—as the saying is, if he took the dirt out o' the road, it id turn to money wid him; and so, in coorse of time, he bought great estates, and was a great man entirely—not a greater in Ireland, throth."

Fearing here a digression on landed interest, I interrupted him, to ask how he and the fiend settled their accounts at last?

"Oh, Sir, you'll hear that all in good time. Sure enough it's terrible, and wondherful it is at the ind, and mighty improvin'—glory be to God!"

"Is that what you say," said I, in surprise, "because a wicked and deluded man lost his soul to the tempter!"

"Oh, the Lord forbid, your honour; but don't be impatient, and you'll hear all. They say, at last, after many years of prosperity, that the old Colonel got stricken in years, and he began to have misgivins in his conscience for his wicked doins, and his heart was heavy as the fear of death came upon him; and sure enough, while he had such murnful thoughts, the Divil kem to him, and tould him *he should go wid him.*

"Well, to be sure the owld man was frekened, but he plucked up his courage and his cuteness, and towld the Divil, in a bantherin' way, jokin' like, that he had partic'lar business thin, that he was goin' to a party, and hoped an *owld friend* wouldn't inconvaynience him, that a-way—."

"Well," said I, laughing at the "put off" of *going to a party*, "the Devil, of course, would take no excuse, and carried him off in a flash of fire?"

"Oh, no, Sir," answered the old man, in something of a reproving, or, at least, offended tone—"that's the finish, I know very well, of many a story, such as we're talkin' of, but that's not the way of this, *which is thruth every word*, what I tell you—."

"I beg your pardon for the interruption," said I.

"No offince in life, Sir," said the venerable chronicler, who was now deep in his story, and would not be stopped.

"Well, Sir," continued he, "the Divil said he'd call the next day and that he must be ready; and sure enough in the evenin' he kem to him; and when the Colonel seen him, he reminded him of his bargain that as long as he could give him some work he couldn't do, he wasn't obleeged to go.

"'That's thrue,' says the Divil.

"'I'm glad you're as good as your word, any how,' says the Colonel.

"'I never bruk my word yit,' says the owld chap, cocking up his horns consaitedly— 'honour bright,' says he.

"'Well, then,' says the Colonel, 'build me a mill, down there, by the river,' says he, 'and let me have it finished by to-morrow mornin'.'

"'Your will is my pleasure,' says the owld chap, and away he wint; and the Colonel thought he had nick'd Owld Nick at last, and wint to bed quite aisy in his mind.

"But, *jewel machree*; sure the first thing he heerd the next mornin' was, that the whole counthry round was runnin' to see a fine bran new mill, that was an the river side, where, the evening before, not a thing at all at all but rushes was standin', and all, of coorse, wonderin' what brought it there; and some sayin' 'twas not lucky, and many more throubled in their mind, but one and all agreein' it was no *good*; and that's the very mill forninst you, that you were takin' aff, and the stone that I noticed is a remarkable one—a big coign-stone—that they say the Divil himself laid first, and has the mark of four fingers and a thumb an it, to this day.

"But when the Colonel heerd it, he was more throubled than any, of coorse, and began to conthrive what else he could think iv, to keep himself out iv the claws of the *owld one*. Well, he often heerd tell that there was one thing the Divil never could do, and I dar say you heerd it too, Sir,—that is, that he couldn't make a rope out of the sands of the sae; and so when the *owld one* kem to him the next day, and said his job was done, and that now the mill was built, he must either tell him somethin' else he wanted done, or come away wid him.

"So the Colonel said he saw it was all over wid him; 'but,' says he, 'I wouldn't like to go wid you alive, and sure it's all the same to you, alive or dead?'

"'Oh, that won't do,' says his frind; 'I can't wait no more;' says he.

"'I don't want you to wait, my dear frind,' says the Colonel; 'all I want is, that you'll be plased to kill me, before you take me away.'

"'With pleasure,' says Ould Nick.

"'But will you promise me my choice of dyin' one partic'lar way?' says the Colonel.

"'Half a dozen ways, if it plazes you,' says he.

"'You're mighty obleegin',' says the Colonel; 'and so,' says he, 'I'd rather die by bein' hanged with a rope *made out of the sands of the sae*,' says he, lookin' mighty knowin' at the *ould fellow.*

"'I've always one about me,' says the Divil, 'to obleege my frinds,' says he; and with that, he pulls out a rope made of sand, sure enough.

"'Oh, it's game you're makin',' says the Colonel, growin' as white as a sheet.

"'The *game is mine*, sure enough,' says the mild fellow, grinnin' with a terrible laugh.

"'That's not a sand-rope at all,' says the Colonel.

"'Isn't it?' says the Divil, hittin' him acrass the face with the ind iv the rope, and the sand (for it was made of sand, sure enough) went into one of his eyes, and made the tears come with the pain.

"'That bates all I ever seen or heerd,' says the Colonel, sthrivin' to rally, and make another offer—'is there any thing you *can't* do?'

"'Nothin' you can tell me,' says the Divil, 'so you may as well lave off your palaverin', and come along at wanst.'

"'Will you give me one more offer,' says the Colonel.

"'You don't deserve it,' says the Divil, 'but I don't care if I do;' for you see, Sir, he was only playin' wid him, and tantalising the ould sinner.

"'All fair,' says the Colonel, and with that he ax'd like could he stop a woman's tongue.

"'Thry me,' says Ould Nick.

"'Well then,' says the Colonel, 'make my lady's tongue be quiet for the next month, and I'll thank you.'

"'She'll never throuble you agin,' says Ould Nick; and, with that, the Colonel heerd roarin' and cryin', and the door of his room was thrown open, and in ran his daughter, and fell down at his feet, telling him her mother had just dhropped dead.

"The minit the door opened, the Divil runs and hides himself behind a big elbow chair; and the Colonel was frekened almost out of his siven sinses, by raison of the sudden death of his poor lady, let alone the jeopardy he was in himself, seein' how the Divil had *forestall'd* him every way; and after ringin' his bell, and callin' to his servants, and recoverin' his daughther out of her faint, he was goin' away wid her out o' the room, whin the Divil caught howld of him by the skirt of the coat, and the Colonel was obleeged to let his daughter be carried out by the sarvants, and shut the doer afther them.

"'Well,' says the Divil, and he grinn'd and wagg'd his tail, and all as one as a dog when he's plaised—'what do you say now?' says he.

"'Oh,' says the Colonel, 'only lave me alone antil I bury my poor wife,' says he, 'and I'll go with you then, you villian,' says he.

"'Don't call names,' says the Divil; 'you had better keep a civil tongue in your head,' says he; 'and it doesn't become a gintleman to forget good manners.'

"Well, Sir, to make a long story short, the Divil purtended to let him off, out of kindness, for three days, antil his wife was buried; but the raison of it was this, that when the lady his daughter fainted, he loosened the clothes about her throat, and in pulling some of her dhress away, he tuk off a goold chain that was an her neck and put in his pocket, and the chain had a diamond crass on it, (the Lord be praised!) and the Divil darn't touch him while he had the *sign of the crass* about him.

"Well, the poor Colonel, God forgive him, was grieved for the loss of his lady, and she had an *illigant berrin*—and they say, that when the prayers was readin' over the dead, the ould Colonel took it to heart like any thing, and the word o' God kem home to his poor sinful sowl at last.

"Well, Sir, to make a long story short, the ind if it was, that for the three days o' grace that was given to him the poor deluded ould sinner did nothin' at all but read the Bible from mornin' till night, and bit or sup didn't pass his lips all the time, he was so intint upon the holy book, but sat up in an ould room in the far ind of the house, and bid no one disturb him an no account and struv to make his heart bould with the words iv life; and sure it was somethin' strinthened him at last, though as the time drew nigh that the *inimy* was to come, he didn't feel aisy; and no wondher; and, by dad, the three days was past and gone in no time, and the story goes that at the dead hour o' the night, when the poor sinner was readin' away as fast as he could, my jew'l, his heart jumped up to his mouth, at gettin' a tap on the shoulder.

"'Oh, murther!' says he, 'who's there?' for he was afeard to look up.

"'It's me,' says the *ould one*, and he stood right forninst him, and his eyes like coals o' fire, lookin' him through, and he said, with a voice that a'most split his ould heart, 'Come!' says he.

"'Another day,' cried out the poor Colonel.

"'Not another hour,' says Sat'n.

"'Half an hour?'

"'Not a quarther,' says the Divil, grinnin', with a bitther laugh— 'give over your readin', I bid you,' says he, 'and come away wid me.'

"'Only gi' me a few minits,' says he.

"'Lave aff your palavering,' you snakin' ould sinner,' says Sat'n; 'you know you're bought and sould to me, and a purty bargain I have o' you, you ould baste,' says he—'so come along at wanst,' and he put out his claw to ketch him; but the Colonel tuk a fast hould o' the Bible, and begg'd hard that he'd let him alone, and wouldn't harm him antil the bit o' candle that was just blinkin' in the socket before him was burned out.

"'Well, have it so, you dirty coward,' says Ould Nick—and with that he spit an him.

"But the poor ould Colonel didn't lose a minit (for he was cunnin' to the ind), but snatched the little taste o' candle that was forninst him, out o' the candlestick, an puttin' it an the holy book before him, he shut down the cover of it, and quinched the light. With that, the Divil gave a roar like a bull, and vanished in a flash o' fire, and the poor Colonel fainted away in his chair; but the sarvants heerd the noise (for the Divil tore aff the roof o' the house when he left it), and run into the room, and brought their master to himself agin. And from that day out he was an althered man, and used to have the Bible read to him every day, for he couldn't read himself any more, by raison of losin' his eyesight, when the Divil hit him with the rope of sand in the face, and afther spit an him—for the sand wint into one eye, and he lost the other that-a-way, savin' your presence.

"So you see, Sir, afther all, the Colonel, undher heaven, was too able for the Divil, and by readin' the good book his sowl was saved, and (glory be to God) *isn't that mighty improvin'?*"

The foregoing tale, we believe, is somewhat common to the legendary lore of other countries—at least, there is a German legend built on a similar foundation. We hope, however, it may not be considered totally uninteresting, our effort being to show the different styles his sable majesty has of cutting his capers in Germany and in Ireland.

1. An allusion to a post of importance that was betrayed in some of the battles between William III and James II.

THE GRIDIRON

OR
PADDY MULLOWNEY'S TRAVELS
IN FRANCE

Soldier—Boskos thromuldo boskos.
Parolles—I know you are the Musko's regiment.
Soldier—Bokos vauvado.
Parolles—I understand thee, and can speak thy tongue.
ALL'S WELL THAT ENDS WELL

MATHEWS, IN HIS "TRIP TO America," gives a ludicrous representation of an Irishman who has left his own country on the old-fashioned speculation of "seeking his fortune," and who, after various previous failures in the pursuit, at length goes into the back settlement with the intention of becoming interpreter-general between the Yankees and the Indian tribes; but the Indians reject his proffered service, "*the poor ignorant craytures,*" as he himself says, "*just because* he did not understand the language." We are told, moreover, that Goldsmith visited the land of dykes and dams, for the purpose of teaching the Hollanders *English*, quite overlooking (until his arrival in the country made it obvious), that he did not know a word of *Dutch* himself. I have prefaced the following story thus, in the hope that the "*precedent,*" which covers so many absurdities in law, may be considered available by the *author*, as well as the *suitor*, and may serve a turn in the court of criticism, as well as in the common pleas.

A certain old gentleman in the west of Ireland, whose love of the ridiculous quite equalled his taste for claret and fox-hunting, was wont, upon certain festive occasions, when opportunity offered, to amuse his friends by *drawing out* one of his servants, who was exceeding fond of what he termed his "*thravels,*" and in whom, a good deal of whim, some queer stories, and perhaps, more than all, long and faithful services, had established a right of loquacity. He was one of those few trusty and privileged domestics, who, if his master unheedingly uttered a rash thing in a fit of passion, would venture to set him right. If the squire said, "I'll turn that rascal off," my friend Pat would say, "throth you won't, Sir;" and Pat was always right, for if any altercation arose upon the "subject matter in hand," he was sure to throw in some good reason, either from former services—general good conduct—or the delinquent's "wife and childher," that always turned the scale.

But I am digressing: on such merry meetings as I have alluded to, the master, after making certain "approaches," as a military man would say, as the preparatory steps in laying siege to some *extravaganza* of his servant, might, perchance, assail Pat thus: "By-the-bye, Sir John (addressing a distinguished guest), Pat has a very curious story which something you told me to-day reminds me of. You remember, Pat (turning to the man, evidently pleased at the notice thus paid to himself),—you remember that queer adventure you had in France?"

"Throth I do, Sir," grins forth Pat.

"What!" exclaims Sir John, in feigned surprise, "was Pat ever in France?"

"Indeed he was," cries mine host; and Pat adds, "ay, and farther, plaze your honour."

"I assure you, Sir John," continues my host, "Pat told me much, respecting the ignorance of the French."

"Indeed!" rejoins the baronet, "really, I always supposed the French to be a most accomplished people."

"Throth then, they're not, Sir," interrupts Pat.

"Oh, by no means," adds mine host, shaking his head emphatically.

"I believe, Pat, 'twas when you were crossing the Atlantic?" says the master, turning to Pat with a seductive air, and leading into the "full and true account"—(for Pat had thought fit to visit *North Amerikay*, for "a raison he had," in the autumn of the year 'ninety-eight).

"Yes, Sir," says Pat, "the broad Atlantic,"—a favourite phrase of his, which he gave with a brogue as broad, almost, as the Atlantic itself.

"It was the time I was lost in crassin' the broad Atlantic, a comin' home," began Pat, decoyed into the recital; "whin the winds began to blow, and the sae to rowl, that you'd think the *Colleen dhas* (that was her name), would not have a mast left but what would rowl out of her.

"Well, sure enough, the masts went by the boord, at last, and the pumps were choak'd (divil choak them for that same), and av coorse the wather gained an us; and troth, to be filled with wather is neither good for man or baste; and she was sinkin' fast, settlin' down, as the sailors call it; and faith I never was good at settlin' down in my life, and I liked it then less nor ever; accordingly we prepared for the worst, and put out the boat, and got a sack o' bishkets, and a cashk o' pork, and a kag o' wather, and a thrifle o' rum aboord, and any other little matthers we could think iv in the mortial hurry we wor in—and fait there was no time to be lost, for my darlint, the *Colleen dhas* went down like a lump o' lead, afore we wor many strokes o' the oar away from her.

"Well, we dhrifted away all that night, and next mornin' we put up a blanket an the ind av a pole as well as we could, and then we sailed iligant; for we darn't show a titch o' canvass the night before, bekase it was blowin' like bloody murther, savin' your presence, and sure it's the wondher of the world we worn't swally'd alive by the ragin' sae.

"Well, away we wint, for more nor a week, and nothin' before our two good-lookin' eyes but the canophy iv heaven, and the wide ocean—the broad Atlantic—not a thing was to be seen but the sae and the sky; and though the sae and the sky is mighty purty things in themselves, throth they're no great thing when you've nothin' else to look at for a week together—and the barest rock in the world, so it was land, would be more welkim. And then, soon enough throth, our provisions began to run low, the bishkits, and the wather, and the rum—throth *that* was gone first of all—God help uz—and, oh! it was thin that starvation began to stare us in the face—'Oh, murther, murther, captain darlint,' says I, 'I wish we could see land any where,' says I.

"'More power to your elbow, Paddy, my boy,' says he, 'for sitch a good wish, and throth it's myself wishes the same.'

"'Oh,' says I, 'that it may plaze you, sweet queen iv heaven, supposing it was only a dissolute island,' says I, 'inhabited wid Turks, sure they wouldn't be such bad Christhans as to refuse us a bit and a sup.'

"'Whisht, whisht, Paddy,' says the captain, 'don't be talkin' bad of any one,' says he; 'you don't know how soon you may want a good word put in for yourself, if you should be called to quarthers in th' other world all of a suddint,' says he.

"'Thrue for you, captain darlint,' says I—I called him darlint, and made free wid him, you see, bekase disthress makes uz all equal—'thrue for you, captain jewel—God betune uz and harm, I owe no man any spite'—and throth that was only thruth. Well, the last bishkit was sarved out, and by gor the *wather itself* was all gone at last, and we passed the night mighty cowld—well, at the brake o' day the sun riz most beautiful out o' the waves, that was as bright as silver and as clear as crysthal. But it was only the more cruel upon us, for we wor beginnin' to feel *terrible* hungry; when all at wanst I thought I spied the land—by gor I thought I felt my heart up in my throat in a minnit, and 'Thunder an turf, captain,' says I, 'look to leeward,' says I.

"'What for?' says he.

"'I think I see the land,' says I. So he ups with his bring-'m-near—(that's what the sailors call a spy-glass, Sir), and looks out, and, sure enough, it was.

"'Hurra!' says he, 'we're all right now; pull away, my boys,' says he.

"'Take care you're not mistaken,' says I; 'maybe it's only a fog-bank, captain darlint,' says I.

"'Oh no,' says he, 'it's the land in airnest.'

"'Oh then, whereabouts in the wide world are we, captain?' says I, 'maybe it id be in *Roosia*, or *Proosia*, or the Garman Oceant,' says I.

"'Tut, you fool,' says he—for he had that consaited way wid im—thinkin' himself cleverer nor any one else—'tut, you fool,' says he, 'that's *France*,' says he.

"'Tare an ouns,' says I, 'do you tell me so? and how do you know it's France it is, captain dear?' says I.

"'Bekase thi is the Bay o' Bishky we're in now,' says he.

"'Throth I was thinkin' so myself,' says I, 'by the rowl it has; for I often heerd av it in regard of that same;' and throth the likes av it I never seen before nor since, and, with the help o' God, never will.

"Well, with that, my heart began to grow light; and when I seen my life was safe, I began to grow twice hungrier nor ever—'so,' says I 'captain jewel, wish we had a gridiron.'

"'Why then,' says he, 'thunder an turf,' says he, 'what puts a gridiron into your head?'

"'Bekase I'm starvin' with the hunger,' says I.

"'And sure, bad luck to you,' says he, 'you couldn't ate a gridiron,' says he, 'barrin' you wor a *pelican o' the wildherness*,' says he.

"'Ate a gridiron!' says I; 'och, in throth I'm not sich a *gommoch* all out as that, any how. But sure, if we had a gridiron, we could dress a beef-stake,' says I.

"'Arrah! but where's the beef-stake?' says he.

"'Sure, couldn't we cut a slice aff the pork,' says I.

"'Be gor, I never thought o' that,' says the captain. 'You're a clever fellow, Paddy,' says he, laughin'.

"'Oh, there's many a thrue word said in joke,' says I.

"'Thrue for you, Paddy,' says he.

"'Well then,' says I, 'if you put me a shore there beyant,' (for we were nearin' the land all the time,) 'and sure I can ax thim for to lind me the loan of a gridiron,' says I.

"'Oh by gor, the butther's comin' out o' the stirabout in airnest now,' says he, 'you gommoch,' says he, 'sure I towld you before that's France—and sure they they're all furriners¹ there,' says the captain.

"'Well,' says I, 'and how do you know but I'm as good a furriner myself as any o' thim.'

"'What do you mane?' says he.

"'I mane,' says I, 'what I towld you, that I'm as good a furriner myself as any o' thim.'

"'Make me sinsible,' says he.

"'By dad, maybe that's more nor me, or greater nor me, could do,' says I—and we all began to laugh at him, for I thought I'd pay him off for his bit o' consait about the Garman Oceant.

"'Lave aff your humbuggin',' says he, 'I bid you, and tell me what it is you mane, at all at all.'

"'*Parly voo frongsay*,' says I.

"'Oh, your humble sarvant,' says he; 'why, by gor, you're a scholar, Paddy.'

"'Throth, you may say that,' says I.

"'Why, you're a clever fellow, Paddy,' says the captain, jeerin' like.

"'You're not the first that said that,' says I, 'whether you joke or no.'

"'Oh, but, I'm in airnest,' says the captain—'and do you tell me, Paddy,' says he, 'that you spake Frinch?'

"'*Parly voo frongsay*,' says I.

"'By gor, that bangs Banagher, and all the world knows Banagher bangs the divil—I never met the likes o' you, Paddy,' says he—'pull away, boys, and put Paddy ashore, and maybe we won't get a good bellyful before long.'

"So, with that, it was no sooner said nor done—they pulled away, and got close into shore in less than no time, and run the boat up in a little creek, and a beautiful creek it was, with a lovely white sthrand—an iligant place for ladies to bathe in the summer; and out I got—and it's stiff enough in my limbs I was, afther bein' cramp'd up in the boat, and perished with the cowld and hunger; but I conthrived to scramble on, one way or t'other, tow'rds a little bit iv a wood that was close to the shore, and the smoke curlin' out of it, quite timptin' like.

"'By the powdhers o' war, I'm all right,' says I; 'there's a house there;'—and sure enough there was, and a parcel of men, women, and childher, ating their dinner round a table, quite convaynient. And so I wint up to the door, and I thought I'd be very civil to thim, as I heerd the Frinch was always mighty p'lite intirely—and I thought I'd show them I knew what good manners was.

"So I took aff my hat, and, making a low bow, says I, 'God save all here,' says I.

"Well, to be sure, they all stopt ating at wanst, and begun to stare at me—and, faith, they almost look'd me out o' countenance; and I thought to myself it was not good manners at all—more betoken from furriners, which they call so mighty p'lite; but I never minded that, in regard o' wantin' the gridiron; and so say I, 'I beg your pardon,' says I, 'for the liberty I take, but it's only bein' in disthress in regard of ating' says I, 'that I make bowld to throuble ye; and if you could lind me the loan of agridiron,' says I, 'I'd be entirely obleeged to ye.'

"By gor, they all stared at me twice worse nor before; and with that, says I, (knowin' what was in their minds,) 'indeed, it's thrue for you,' says I—'I'm tatthered to pieces, and God knows I look quare enough—but it's by raison of the storm,' says I, 'which dhruv us ashore here below, and we're all starvin',' says I.

"So then they began to look at each other agin; and myself, seeing at wanst dirty thoughts was in their heads, and that they tuk me for a poor beggar, comin' to crave charity—with that, says I, 'Oh! not at all,' says I, 'by no manes—we have plenty o' mate ourselves, there below, and we'll dhress it,' says I, 'if you would be plased to lind us the loan of a gridiron,' say I, makin' a low bow.

"Well, Sir, with that, throth they stared at me twice worse nor ever—and faith, I began to think that maybe the captain was wrong, and that it was not France at all at all; and so says I, ' I beg pardon, Sir,' says I, to a fine ould man, with a head of hair as white as silver— 'maybe I'm undher a mistake,' says I; 'but I thought I was in France, Sir; aren't you furriners?' says I—'*Parly voo frongsay?*'

"'We munseer,' says he.

"'Then would you lind me the loan of a gridiron,' says I, 'if you plase?'

"Oh, it was thin that they stared at me as if I had siven heads; and, faith, myself began to feel flusthered like, and onaisy—and so says I, makin' a bow and scrape agin, 'I know it's a liberty I take, Sir,' says I, 'but it's only in the regard of bein' cast away; and if you plase, Sir,' says I, '*Parly voo frongsay?*'

"'We munseer,' says he, mighty sharp.

"'Then would you lind me the loan of a gridiron?' says I, 'and you'll obleege me.'

"Well, Sir, the ould chap began to munseer me; but the divil a bit of a gridiron he'd gi' me; and so I began to think they wor all neygars, for all their fine manners; and throth my blood begun to rise, and says I, 'By my sowl, if it was you was in disthriss,' says I, 'and if it was to ould Ireland you kem, it's not only the gridiron they'd give you, if you ax'd it, but something to put an it too, and the dhrop o' dhrink into the bargain, and *cead mile failte.*'

"Well, the word *cead mile failte* seemed to sthreck his heart, and the ould chap cocked his ear, and so I thought I'd giv him another offer, and make him sinsible at last; and so says I, wanst more, quite slow, that he might undherstand—'*Parly—voo—frongsay*, munseer?'

"'We munseer,' says he.

"'Then lind me the loan of a gridiron,' says I, 'and bad scram to you.'

"Well, bad win to the bit of it he'd gi' me, and the ould chap begins bowin' and scrapin', and said something or other about a long tongs.[2]

"'Phoo!—the divil sweep yourself and your tongs,' says I, 'I don't want a tongs at all at all but can't you listen to raison,' says I—'*Parly voo frongsay?*'

"'We munseer.'

"'Then lind the loan of a gridiron,' says I, 'and howld your prate.'

"Well, what would you think but he shook his owld noddle, as nuch as to say he wouldn't; and so says I, 'Bad cess to the likes o'that

I ever seen—throth if you wor in my country it's not that-a-way they'd use you, owld sinner,' says I, 'the devil a longer I'll darken your door.'

"So he seen I was vex'd, and I thought, as I was turnin' away, I seen him begin to relint, and that his conscience throubled him; and, says I, turnin' back, 'Well, I'll give you one chance more—you ould thief—are you a Chrishthan at all at all? are you a furriner?' says I, 'that all the world calls so p'lite. Bad luck to you, do you undherstand your own language?—*Parly voo frongsay?*' says I.

"'We munseer,' says he.

"'Then thunder an turf,' says I, 'will you lind me the loan of a gridiron?'

"Well, Sir, the divil resave the bit of it he'd gi' me—and so with that, the 'curse o' the hungry an you, you ould negarly villian,' says I: 'the back o' my hand and the sowl o' my fut to you, that you may want a gridiron yourself yit,' says I; 'and wherever I go, high and low, rich and poor, shall hear o' you,' says I; and with that I left them there, Sir, and kem away—and in throth it's often sense that *I thought that it was remarkable.*"

1.   Foreigners.
2.   Some mystification of Paddy's touching the French *n'entends*.

PADDY THE PIPER

Dogberry—Marry, Sir, they have committed false reports; moreover, they have spoken untruths; secondarily, they are slanderers; sixthly and lastly they have belied a lady; thirdly, they have verified unjust things; and to conclude, they are lying knaves.

MUCH ADO ABOUT NOTHING

THE ONLY INTRODUCTION I SHALL attempt to the following "*extravaganza,*" is, to request the reader to be delivered by a frolicking Irish peasant, in the richest brogue, and most dramatic manner.

"I'll tell you, Sir, a mighty quare story, and it's as thrue as I'm standin' here, and that's no lie:—

"It was in the time of the '*ruction,*[1] whin the long summer days, like many a fine fellow's precious life, was cut short by raison of the martial law—that wouldn't let a dacent boy be out in the evenin', good or bad; for whin the day's work was over, divil a one of uz dar go to meet a frind over a glass, or a girl at the dance, but must go home, and shut ourselves up, and never budge, nor rise latch, nor dhraw boult, antil the morning kem agin.

"Well, to come to my story:—'Twas afther night fall, and we wor sittin' round the fire, and the praties wor boilin', and the noggins of butthermilk was standin' ready for our suppers, whin a knock kem to the door.

"'Whisht!' says my father, 'here's the sojers come upon us now,' says he; 'bad luck to thim, the villians, I'm afeared they seen a glimmer of the fire through the crack in the door,' says he.

"'No,' says my mother, 'for I'm afther hangin' an ould sack and my new petticoat agin it, a while ago.'

"'Well, whisht, any how,' says my father, 'for there's a knock agin;' and we all held our tongues till another thump kem to the door.

"'Oh, it's a folly to purtind any more,' says my father—'they're too cute to be put off that-a-way,' says he. 'Go, Shamus,' says he to me, 'and see who's in it.'

"'How can I see who's in it in the dark?' says I.

"'Well,' says he, 'light the candle thin, and see who's in it, but don't open the door, for your life, barrin' they brake it in,' says he, 'exceptin' to the sojers, and spake thim fair, if it's thim.'

"So with that I wint to the door, and there was another knock.

"'Who's here?' says I.

"'It's me' says he.

"'Who are you?' says I.

"'A frind' says he.

"'*Baithershin,*' says I,—'who are you at all?'

"'Arrah! don't you know me?' says he.

"'Divil a taste,' says I.

"'Sure I'm Paddy the Piper,' says he.

"'Oh, thunder an turf,' says I, 'is it you, Paddy, that's in it?'

"'Sorra one else,' says he.

"'And what brought you at this hour?' says I.

"'By gar,' says he, 'I didn't like goin' the roun' by the road,' says he, 'and so I kem the short cut, and that's whet delayed me,' says he.

"'Oh, bloody wars!' says I—'Paddy, I wouldn't be in your shoes for the king's ransom,' says I; 'for you know yourself it's a hangin' matther to be cotched out these times.' says I.

"'Sure I know that,' says he, 'God help me; and that's what I kem to you for,' says he; 'and let me in for ould acquaintance sake,' says poor Paddy.

"'Oh, by this and that,' says I, 'I darn't open the door for the wide world; and sure you know it; and throth, if the Husshians or the Yeos[2] ketches you,' says I, 'they'll murther you, as sure as your name's Paddy.'

"'Many thanks to you,' says he, 'for your good intintions; but, plaze the pigs, I hope it's not the likes o' that is in store for me, any how.'

"'Faix then,' says I 'you had bedther lose no time in hidin' yourself,' says I; 'for, throth I tell you, it's a short thrial and a long rope the Husshians would be afther givin' you—for they've no justice, and less marcy, the villians!'

"'Faith thin, more's the raison you should let me in, Shamus,' says poor Paddy.

"'It's a folly to talk,' says I, ' I darn't open the door.'

"'Oh then, millia murther?' says Paddy, 'what'll become of me at all at all,' says he.

"'Go aff into the shed,' says I, 'behin' the house, where the cow is, and there there's an iligant lock o' straw, that you may go sleep in,' says I, 'and a fine bed it id be for a lord, let alone a piper.'

"'So off Paddy set to hide in the shed, and throth it wint to our hearts to refuse him, and turn him away from the door, more by token when the praties was ready—for sure the bit and the sup is always welkim to the poor thraveller. Well, we all wint to bed, and Paddy hid himself in the cow-house; and now I must tell you how it was with Paddy:—

"You see, afther sleeping for some time, Paddy wakened up, think' it was morning', but it wasn't mornin' at all, but only the light o' the moon that desaved him; but at all evints, he wanted to be stirrin' airly, bekase he was goin' off to the town hard by, it bein' fair day, to pick up a few ha'pence with his pipes—for the devil a bedther piper was in all the counthry round, nor Paddy; and every one gave it up to Paddy that he was iligant an the pipes, and played 'Jinny bang'd the Weaver,' beyant tellin', and the 'Hare in the Corn,' that you'd think the very dogs was mad.

"Well, as I was sayin', he set off to go to the fair, and he wint meandherin' along through the fields, but he didn't go far, antil

climbin' up through a hedge, when he was comin' out at t'other
side, his head kem plump agin somethin' that made the fire flash out
out iv his eyes. So with that he looks up—and what do you think
it was, Lord be marciful to uz, but a corpse hangin' out of a branch
of a three.

"'Oh, the top o' the mornin' to you, Sir,' says Paddy, 'and is that the
way with you, my poor fellow? throth you tuk a start out o' me,' says
poor Paddy; and 'twas thrue for him, for it would make the heart
of a stouter man nor Paddy jump, to see the like, and to think of a
Chrishthan crathur being hanged up, all as one as a dog.

"Now, 'twas the rebels that hanged this chap—bekase, you see,
the corpse had got clothes an him, and that's the raison that one
might know it was the rebels—by raison that the Husshians and the
Orangemen never hanged any body wid good clothes an him, but
only the poor and definceless crathurs, like uz so, as I said before,
Paddy knew well it was the boys that done it; 'and,' says Paddy, eyin'
the corpse, 'by my sowl, thin, but you have a beautiful pair o' boots
an you,' says he, 'and it's what I'm thinkin' you won't have any great
use for thim no more; and sure it's a shame to the likes o' me,' says
he, 'the best piper in the sivin counties, to he trampin' wid a pair of
ould brogues not worth three traneeens, and a corpse with such an
iligant pair o' boots, that wants some one to wear thim. So, with that,
Paddy lays hould of him by the boots, and began a pullin' at thim,
but they wor mighty stiff; and whether it was by raison of their bein'
so tight, or the branch of the three a-jiggin' up an down, all as one
as a weighdee buckettee, an not lettin' Paddy cotch any right hoult
o' thim—he could get no *advantage* o'thim at all— and at last he gev
it up, and was goin' away, whin lookin' behind him agin, the sight
of the iligant fine boots was too much for him, and he turned back,
determined to have the boots, any how, by fair means or foul; and
I'm loath to tell you how he got thim—for indeed it was a dirty
turn, and throth it was the only dirty turn I ever saw Paddy to be
guilty av; and you see it was this a-way; 'pon my sowl, he pulled
out a big knife, and, by the same token, it was a knife with a fine
buck-handle, and a murtherin' big blade, that an uncle o'mine, that

was a gardener at the lord's, made Paddy a prisint av; and, more by token, it was not the first mischief that knife done, for it cut love between thim, that was the best of frinds before; and sure 'twas the wondher of every one, that two knowledgeable men, that ought to know betther, would do the likes, and give and take sharp steel in frindship; but I'm forgettin'—well, he outs with his knife, and what does he do, but he cuts off the legs of the corpose; 'and', says he, 'I can take off the boots at my convaynience;' and throth it was, as I said before, a dirty turn.

"Well, Sir, he tuck'd the legs undher his arms, and at that minit the moon peeped out from behind a cloud—'Oh! is it there you are?' says he to the moon, for he was an impidint chap—and thin, seein' that he made a mistake, and that the moon-light deceaved him, and that it wasn't the airly dawn, as he conceaved; and bein' friken'd for fear himself might be cotched and trated like the poor corpose he was afther a malthreating, if *he* was found walking the counthry at that time—by far, he turned about, and walked back agin to the cow-house, and, hidin' the corpse's legs in the sthraw, Paddy wint to sleep agin. But what do you think? the divil a long Paddy was there antil the sojers came in airnest, and, by the powers, they carried off Paddy—and faith it was only sarvin' him right for what he done to the poor corpse.

"Well, whin the mornin' kem, my father says to me, 'Go, Shamus,' says he, 'to the shed, and bid poor Paddy come in, and take share o' the praties, for, I go bail, he's ready for his breakquest by this, any how?'

"Well, out I wint to the cow-house, and called out 'Paddy!' and afther callin' three or four times, and gettin' no answer, I wint in, and called agin, and divil an answer I got still. 'Blood-an-agers!' says I, 'Paddy, where are you at all at all?' and so, castin' my eyes about the shed, I seen two feet sticking out from undher the hape o' straw— 'Musha! thin,' says I, 'bad luck to you, Paddy, but you're fond of a warm corner, and maybe you haven't made yourself as snug as a flay in a blanket? but I'll disturb your dhrames, I'm thinkin',' says I, and with that I laid hould of his heels (as I thought, God help me), and givin' a good pull to waken him, as I intinded, away I wint, head over heels, and my brains was a'most knocked out agin the wall.

"Well, whin I recovered myself, there I was, an the broad o' my back, and two things stickin' out o' my hands like a pair o' Husshian's horse-pist'ls—and I thought the sight 'id lave my eyes, when I seen they wor two mortial legs.

"My jew'l, I threw them down like a hot pratee, and jumpin' up, I roared out millia murther. 'Oh, you murtherin' villian,' says I, shakin' my fist at the cow—'Oh, you unnath'ral *baste*,' says I, 'you've ate poor Paddy, you thievin' cannible, you're worse than a neygar,' says I; 'and bad luck to you, how dainty you are, that nothin' 'id serve you for your supper, but the best piper in Ireland. *Weirasthru! weirasthru!* what'll the whole countthry say to such an unnath'ral murther? and you lookin' as innocent there as a lamb, and atin' your hay as quite as if nothin' happened.' With that, I run out—for, throth, I didn't like to be near her—and, goin' into the house, I tould them all about it.

"'Arrah! be aisy,' says my father.

"' Bad luck to the lie I tell you,' says I.

"'Is it ate Paddy?' says they.

"'Divil a doubt of it,' says I.

"'Are you sure, Shamus?' says my mother.

"'I wish I was as sure of a new pair o' brogues,' says I. 'Bad luck to the bit she has left iv him but his two legs.'

"'And do you tell me she ate the pipes too?' says my father.

"'By gor, I b'lieve so,' says I.

"'Oh, the divil fly away wid her,' says he, 'what a cruel taste she has for music!'

"'Arrah!' says my mother, 'don't be cursin' the cow, that gives the milk to the childher.'

"'Yis, I will,' says my father, 'why shouldn't I curse sich an unnath'ral baste?'

"'You oughtn't to curse any livin' thing that's undher your roof,' says my mother.

"'By my sowl, thin,' says my father, 'she shan't be undher my roof any more; for I'll sind her to the fair this minit,' says he, 'and sell her for whatever she'll bring. Go aff,' says he, 'Shamus, the minit you've ate your breakquest, and dhrive her to the fair.'

"'Throth I don't like to dhrive her,' says I.

"'Arrah, don't be makin' a gommagh of yourself,' says he.

"'Faith, I don't,' says I.

"'Well, like or no like,' says he, 'you must dhrive her.'

"'Sure, father,' says I, 'you could take more care iv her yourself.'

"'That's mighty good,' says he, 'to keep a dog, and bark myself;' and, faith, I rec'llected the sayin' from that hour;—'let me have no more words about it,' says he, 'but be aff wid you.'

"So, aff I wint—and it's no lie I'm tellin', whin I say it was sore agin my will I had any thing to do with sich a villian of a baste. But, howsomever, I cut a brave long wattle, that I might dhrive the manather iv a thief, as she was, without bein' near her, at all at all.

"Well, away we wint along the road, and mighty throng it wuz wid the boys and the girls—and, in short, all sorts, rich and poor, high and low, crowdin' to the fair.

"'God save you,' says one to me.

"'God save you, kindly,' says I.

"'That's a fine baste you're dhrivin',' says he. 'Throth she is,' says I; though God knows it wint agin my heart to say a good word for the likes of her.

"'It's to the fair you're goin', I suppose,' says he, 'with the baste?' (He was a snug-lookin' farmer, ridin' a purty little grey hack).

"'Faith, thin, you're right enough,' says I, 'it is to the fair I'm goin'.

"'What do you expec' for her?' says he

"'Faith, thin, myself doesn't know,' says I—and that was thrue enough, you see, bekase I was bewildered like about the baste, entirely.

"'That's a quare way to be goin' to market,' says he, 'and not to know what you expec' for your baste.'

"'Och', says I—not likin' to let him suspect there was anything wrong wid her—'Och,' says I, in a careless sort of a way, 'sure no one can tell what a baste 'ill bring, antil they come to the fair,' says I, 'and see what price is goin'.'

"'Indeed, that's nath'ral enough,' says he. 'But if you wor bid a fair price before you come to the fair, sure you might as well take it,' says he.

"'Oh, I've no objection in life,' says I. 'Well, thin, what 'ill you ax for her?' says he.

"'Why, thin, I wouldn't like to be onraysonable,' says I—(for the thruth was, you know, I wanted to get rid iv her)—'and so I'll take four pounds for her,' says I, 'and *no less.*'

"'No less!' says he.

"'Why, sure that's chape enough,' says I.

"'Throth it is,' says he; 'and I'm thinkin' it's *too* chape it is,' says he; 'for if there wasn't somethin' the matter, it's not for that you'd be sellin' the fine milch cow, as she is to all appearance.'

"'Indeed thin,' says I, 'upon my conscience, she *is* a fine milch cow.'

"'Maybe,' says he, 'she's gone off her milk, in regard that she doesn't feed well?'

"'Och, by this and that,' says I, 'in regard of feedin' there's not the likes of her in Ireland; so make your mind aisy—and if you like her for the money, you may have her.'

"'Why, indeed, I'm not in a hurry,' says he, 'and I'll wait to see how they go in the fair.'

"'With all my heart,' says I purtendin' to be no ways consarned—but in throth I began to be afeard that the people as seein' somethin' unnath'ral about her, and that we'd never get rid of her, at all at all. At last we kem to the fair, and a great sight o' people was in it throth, you'd think the whole world was there, let alone the standlins o' gingerbread and iligant ribbins, and makins o' beautiful gownds, and pitch-and-toss, and merry-go-rouns, and tints with the best av dhrink in thim, and the fiddles playin' up t' incourage the boys and girls; but I never minded thim at all, but detarmint to sell the thievin' rogue av a cow afore I'd mind any divarshin in life; so an I dhriv her into the thick av the fair, whin all of a suddint, as I kem to the door av a tint, up sthruck the pipes to the tune av 'Tattherin' Jack Welsh,' and, my jew'l, in a minit the cow cock'd her ears, and was makin' a dart at the tint.

"'Oh, murther!' says I, to the boys standin' by, 'hould her,' says I, 'hould her—she ate one piper already, the vagbone, and, bad luck to her, she wants another now.'

"'Is it a cow for to ate a piper?' says one o' thim.

"'Divil a word o' lie in it, for I seen his corpse myself, and nothing' left but the two legs,' says I; 'and it's a folly to be sthrivin' to hide it, for I *see* she'll never lave it aff—as poor Paddy Grogan knows to his cost, Lord be merciful to him.

"'Who's that takin' my name in vain?' says a voice in the crowd; and with that, shovin' the throng a one side, who the divil should I see but Paddy Grogan, to all appearance.

"'Oh, hould him too,' says I; 'keep him av me, for it's not himself at all, but his ghost,' says I 'for he was kilt last night to my sartin knowledge, every inch av him, all to his legs.'

"'Well, Sir, with that, Paddy—for it was Paddy himself, as it kem out afther—fell a laughin', that you'd think his sides 'ad split; and whin he kem to himself, he ups and he tould us how it was, as I towld you already; and the likes av the fun they made av me was beyant tellin', for wrongfully misdoubtin' the poor cow, and layin' the blame iv atin' a piper an her. So we all wint into the tint to have it explained, and by gor it tuk a full gallon o' sper'ts t' explain it; and we dhrank health and long life to Paddy and the cow, and Paddy played that day beyant all tellin', and many a one said the likes was never heerd before nor sence, even from Paddy himself—and av coorse the poor slandhered cow was dhruv home agin, and many a quite day she had wid us afther that; and whin she died, throth my father had sitch a regard for the poor thing, that he had her skinned, and an iligant pair of breeches made out iv her hide, and it's in the fam'ly to this day; and isn't it mighty remarkable it is, what I'm goin' to tell you now, but it's as thrue as I'm here, and from that out, any one that has thim breeches an, the minit a pair o' pipes sthrikes up, they can't rest, but goes jiggin' and jiggin in their sate, and never stops as long as the pipes is playin'—and there," said he, slapping the garment in question that covered his sinewy limb, with a spank of his brawny hand that might have startled nerves more tender than mine—"there, there is the very breeches that's an me now, and a fine pair they are this minit."

The foregoing story I heard related by a gentleman, who said he was not aware to whom the original authorship was attributable.

1.   Insurrection.
2.   Yeomen.

THE PRIEST'S GHOST

Hermione—Pray you sit by us,
 And tell's a tale.
Mamilius—Merry or sad shall't be?
Her. —As merry as you will.
Mam.—A sad tale's best for winter;
 I have one of sprites and goblins.

THE WINTER'S TALE

"A SAD TALE'S BEST FOR winter," saith the epigraph; and it was by the winter's hearth that I heard the following ghost-story, rendered interesting from the air of reverential belief with which it was delivered from the withered lips of an old woman.

Masses for the souls of the dead are among the most cherished items of the Roman Catholic peasant's belief; and it was to prove how sacred a duty the mass for the "soul of the faithful departed" is considered before the eternal judgment-seat, that the tale was told, which I shall endeavour to repeat as my memory will serve, in the words of the original narrator. It was a certain eve of St John, as well as I can remember, that the old dame gave as the date of the supernatural occurrence.

"Whin Mary O'Malley, a friend of my mother's, (God rest her sowl!) and it was herself tould me the story: Mary O'Malley was in the chapel hearin' vespers an the blessed eve o' Saint John, whin, you see, whether it was that she was dhrowsy or tired afther the day's work—for she was all day teddin' the new-cut grass, for 'twas haymakin' sayson: or whether it was *ordered*,[1] and that it was all for the glory of God, and the repose of a throubled sowl, or how it was, it doesn't become me to say; but, howsomever, Mary fell asleep in the chapel, and sound enough she slep' for never a wink she wakened antil every individhial craythur was gone, and the chapel doors was locked. Well, you may be sure it's poor Mary O'Malley was freken'd, and thrimbl'd till she thought she'd ha' died on the spot, and sure no wondher, considerin' she was locked up in a chapel all alone, and in the dark, and no one near her.

"Well, afther a time she recovered herself a little, and she thought there was no use in life in settin' up a phillelew, sthrivin' to make herself heerd, for she knew well no livin' sowl was within call; and so, on a little considheration, whin she got over the first fright at being left alone that-a-way, good thoughts kem into her head to comfort her: and sure she knew she was in God's own house, and that no bad sper't daar come there. So, with that, she knelt down agin, and repeated her crados and pather-and-aves, over and over, antil she felt quite sure in the purtection of hiv'n—and then, wrappin' herself up in her cloak, she thought she might lie down and sthrive to sleep till mornin', whin—'may the Lord keep us!' piously ejaculated the old woman, crossing herself most devoutly, all of a suddint a light shined into the chapel as bright as the light of day, and with that, poor Mary, lookin' up, seen it shinin' out of the door of the vesthry, and immediately, out walked, out of the vesthry, a priest, dhressed in black vestments, a-going slowly up to the althar, he said, 'is there any one here to answer this mass?'

"Well, my poor dear Mary thought the life 'id lave her, for she dhreaded the priest was not of this world, and she couldn't say a word; and whin the priest ax'd three times was there no one there to answer the mass, and got no answer, he walked back agin into the vesthry, and in a minit all was dark agin; but before he wint, Mary thought he looked towards her, and he said she'd never forget the melancholy light of his eyes, and the look he gave her quite pityful like; and she said she never heerd before nor since such a wondherful deep voice.

"Well, Sir, the poor craythur, the minit the sper't was gone—for it was a sper't, God be good to us—that minit the craythur fainted dead away; and so I suppose it was with her, from one faint into another, for she knew nothin' more about any thing antil she recovered and kem to herself in her mother's cabin afther being brought home from the chapel next mornin' whin it was opened for mass, and she was found there.

"I hear thin it was as good as a week before she could lave her bed, she was so overcome by the mortial terror she was in that blessed night, blessed as it was, bein' the eve of a holy saint, and more by token, the manes of givin' repose to a throubled sper't; for you see whin Mary tould what she had seen and heerd to her clargy, his Riverence, undher God, was enlightened to see the maynin' of it all; and the maynin' was this, that he undherstood from hearin' of the priest appearin' in black vestments, that it was for to say mass for the dead that he kem there; and so he supposed that the priest durin' his lifetime had forgot to say a mass for the dead that he was bound to say, and that his poor sowl couldn't have rest antil that mass was said; and that he must walk antil the duty was done.

"So Mary's clargy said to her, that as the knowledge of this was made through her, and as his Riverence said she was chosen, he ax'd her would she go and keep anpther vigil in the chapel, as his Riverence said—and thrue for him—for the repose of a sowl. So Mary bein' a stout girl, and always good, and relyin' on doin' what she thought was her duty in the eyes of God, said she'd watch another night, but hoped she wouldn't be ax'd to stay long in the chapel alone. So the priest tould her 'twould do if she was there a little afore twelve o'clock at night for you know, Sir, that people never appears antil afther twelve, and from that till cock crow; and so accordingly Mary wint on the night of the vigil, and before twelve down she knelt in the chapel, and began a countin' of her beads, and the craythur, she thought every minit was an hour antil she'd be relaysed.

"Well, she wasn't kep' long; for soon the dazzlin' light burst from out of the vesthry door, and the same priest kem out that appeared afore, and in the same melancholy voice he ax'd when he mounted the althar, 'is there any one here to answer this mass?'

"Well, poor Mary sthruv to spake, but the craythur thought her heart was up in her mouth, and not a word could she say; and agin the word was ax'd from the althar, and still she couldn't say aword; but the sweat ran down her forehead as thick as the mountain's rain, and immediately she felt relieved, and the impression was taken aff her heart, like; and so, whin for the third and last time the appearance said, 'Is there *no* one here to answer this mass?' poor Mary mutthered out, 'yis,' as well as she could.

"Oh, often I heerd her say the beautiful sight it was to see the lovely smile upon the face of the sper't, as he turned round, and looked kindly upon her, saying these remarkable words—'It's twenty years,' says he, 'I have been askin' that question, and no one answered till this blessed night, and a blessin' be on her that answered, and now my business on earth is finished;' and with that he vanished, before you could shut your eyes.

"So never say, Sir, it's no good praying for the dead; for you see that even the sowl of a priest couldn't have pace, for forgettin' so holy a thing as a mass for the sowl of the faithful departed."

1.   A reverential mode the Irish have of implying a dispensation of
      providence.

New Potatoes

An Irish Melody

Great cry, and little wool.

OLD SAYING

IN THE MERRY MONTH OF June, or thereabouts, the aforesaid melody may be heard, in all the wailing intonation of its *minor third*, through every street of Dublin.

We Irish are conversational, the lower orders particularly so; and the hawkers, who frequent the streets, often fill the lapses that occur between their cries, by a current conversation with some passing friend, occasionally broken by the deponent "labouring in her calling" and yelling out, "Brave lemons," or "Green *pays*," in some awkward interval, frequently productive of very ludicrous effects.

Such was the case, as I happened to overhear a conversation between Katty, a black-*eyed* dealer in "New pittayatees!" and her friend Sally, who had "Fine fresh Dublin-bay herrings!" to dispose of. Sally, to do her justice, was a very patient hearer, and did not interrupt her friend with her own cry in the least; whether it was from being interested in her friend's little misfortunes, or that Katty was one of those "out-and-outers" in story-telling, who, when once they begin, will never leave off, nor even allow another to edge in a word, as "thin as a sixpence," I will not pretend to say; but certain it is, Katty, in the course of her history, had it all her own way, like "a bull in a chaynee-shop," as she would have said herself.

Such is the manner in which the following sketch from nature came into my possession. That it is altogether slang, I premise; and give all fastidious persons fair warning, that if a picture from low life be not according to their taste, they can leave it unread, rather than blame me for too much fidelity in my outline. So here goes at a *scena*, as the Italians say.

"MY NEW PITTAYATEES!"

Enter Katty, with a grey cloak, a dirty cap, and a black eye; sieve of potatoes *on* her head, and a "trifle o' sper'ts" *in* it. Katty meanders down Patrick Street.

KATTY—*"My new Pittayatees!—My-a-new Pittayatees!—My new—"*

(*Meeting a friend.*)

Sally, darlin', is that you?

SALLY—Throth, it's myself; and what's the matther wid you, Katty?

KAT.—'Deed my heart's bruk, cryin'—*"New pittayatees"*—cryin' afther that vagabone.

SAL.—Is it Mike?

KAT.—Throth, it's himself indeed.

SAL.—And what is it he done?

KAT.—Och! he ruined me with his—*"New pittayatees"*—his goins-an—the ould thing, my dear—

SAL.—Throwin' up his little finger, I suppose?[1]

KAT.—Yis, my darlint: he kem home th' other night, blazin' blind dhrunk, cryin' out—*"New pittay-a-tees!"*—roarin' and bawlin', that you'd think he'd rise the roof aff o' the house.

"Bad luck attend you; bad cess to you, you pot-walloppin' varmint," says he, (maynin' me, i' you plaze) —"wait till I ketch you, you sthrap, and it's I'll give you your fill iv"— '*New pittayatees!*'—"your fill iv a licking, if ever you got it," says he.

So, with that, I knew the villiau was *mulvathered*[2]; let alone the heavy fut o' the miscrayint an the stairs, that a child might know he was done for—"*My new pittayatees!*"—Throth, he was done to a turn, like a mutton-kidney.

SAL.—Musha! God help you, Katty.

KAT.—Oh, wait till you hear the ind o' my—"*New pittayatees!*"— o' my throubles, and it's then you'll open your eyes—"*My new pittayatees!*"

SAL.—Oh, bud I pity you.

KAT.—Oh, wait—wait, my jewel—wait till you hear what became o' my—"*New pittayatees!*"—wait till I tell you the ind of it. Where did I lave aff? Oh, ay, at the stairs.

Well, as he was comin' up stairs, (knowin' how it 'd be,) I thought it best to take care o' my—"*New pittayatees!*"—to take care o' myself; so with that I put the bowlt an the door, betune me and danger, and kep' listenin' at the key-hole; and sure enough, what should I hear but—"*New pittayatees!*"—but the vagabone gropin' his way round the cruked turn in the stair, and tumblin' afther into the hole in the flure an the landin', and whin he come to himself, he gev a thunderin' thump at the door. "Who's there?" says I: says he—"*New pittayatees!*"— "let me in," says he, "you vagabone (swearin' by what I wouldn't mintion), or by this and that, I'll *massacray* you," says he, "within an inch o'—'*New pittayatees!*' within an inch o' your life," says he. "Mikee, darlint," says I, soother'in him.

SAL.—Why would you call sitch a 'tarnal vagabone, darlint?

KAT.—My jew'l, didn't I tell you I thought it best to soother him with—"*New pittayatees!*"—with a tindher word: so, says I, "Mikee, you villian, you're disguised," says I, "you're disguised, dear."

"You lie," says he, "you impident, sthrap, I'm not disguised; but, if I'm disguised itself," says he, "I'll make you know the differ," says he.

Oh! I though the life id lave me, when I heerd him say the word; and with that I put my hand an—"*My new pittayatees!*"—an the latch o' the door, to purvint it from slippin'; and he ups and he gives a wicked kick at the door, and says he, "If you don't let me in this minit," says he, "I'll be the death o' your—'*New pittayatees!*'—o' yourself and your dirty breed," says he. Think o' that, Sally dear, to abuse my relations.

SAL.—Oh, the ruffin.

KAT.—Dirty breed, indeed! By my sowkins, they're as good as his any day in the year, and was never beholden to—"*New pittayatees!*"—to go a beggin' to the mendicity for their dirty—"*New pittayatees!*"—their dirty washins o' pots, and sarvints' lavins, and dogs' bones, all as one as that cruk'd disciple of his mother's cousin's sisther, the ould dhrunken asperseand, as she is.

SAL.—No, in throth, Katty dear.

KAT.—Well, where was I? Oh, ay, I left off at— "*New pittayatees!*"— I left off at my dirty breed. Well, at the word "dirty breed," I knew full well the bad dhrop was up in him—and, faith it's soon and suddint he made me sensible av it, for the first word he said was— "*New pittayatees!*"—the first word he said was to put his shouldher to the door, and in he bursted the door, fallin' down in the middle o' the flure, cryin' out—"*New pittayatees!*"—cryin' out, "bad luck attind you," says he, "how dar' you refuse to lit me into my own house, you sthrap," says he, "agin the law o' the land," says he, scramblin' up on his pins agin, as well as he could; and, as he was risin', says I—"*New pittayatees!*"—says I to him (screeching out loud, that the neighbours in the flure below might hear me,) "Mikee, my darlint," says I.

"Keep the pace, you vagabone," says he; and with that, he hits me a lick av a—"*New pittayatees!*"—a lick av a stick he had in his hand, and down I fell (and small blame to me), down I fell an the flure, cryin'—"*New pittayatees!*"—cryin' out, "Murther! murther!"

SAL.—Oh, the hangin' bone villain!

KAT.—Oh, that's not all! As I was risin', my jew'l, he was goin' to sthrek me again; and with that, I cried out—"Fair play, Mikee," says I; "don't sthrek a man down;" but he wouldn't listen to rayson, and was goin' to hit me agin, whin I put up the child that was in my arms betune me and harm. "Look at your babby, Mikee," says I. "How do I know that, you flag-hoppin' jade," says he (Think o' that, Sally, jew'l—misdoubtin' my virtue, and I an honest woman, as I am. God help me!!!).

SAL.—Oh! Bud you're to be pitied, Katty dear.

KAT.—Well, puttin' up the child betune me and harm, as he was risin' his hand—"Oh!" says I, "Mikee, darlint, don't sthrek the babby;" but, my dear, before the word was out o' my mouth, he struk the babby. (I thought the life 'id lave me). And, iv coorse, the poor babby, that never spuk a word, began to cry—"*New pittayatees!*"— began to cry, and roar, and bawl, and no wondher.

SAL.—Oh, the haythen, to go sthrek the child

KAT.—And, my jew'l, the neighbours in the flure below, hearin' the scrimmage, kem runnin' up the stairs, cryin' out—"*New pittayatees*"—cryin' out, "Watch, watch, Mikee M'Evoy," says they, "would you murther your wife, you villian?" "What's that to you?" says he; "isn't she my own?" says he, "and if I plaze to make her feel the weight o' my—"*New pittayatees*"—the weight o' my fist, what's that to you?" says he; "it's none o' your business, any how, so keep your tongue in your jaw, and your toe in your pump, and 'twill be betther for your—"*New pittayatees*"—'twill be betther for your health, I'm thinkin'," says he; and with that he looked cruked at thim, and squared up to one o' thim—(a poor definceless craythur, a tailor).

"Would you fight your match?" says the poor innocent man.

"Lave my sight," says Mike, "or, by jingo, I'll put a stitch in your side, my jolly tailor," says he.

"Yiv put a stitch in your wig already," says the tailor, "and that'll do for the present writin'."

And with that, Mikee was goin' to hit him with a "*New pittayatee*"—a lift-hander; but he was cotch howld iv before he could let go his blow; and who should stand up forninst him, but—"*My new pittayatees*"—but the tailor's wife (and, by my sowl, it's she that's the sthrapper, and more's the pity she's thrown away upon one o'

the sort); and says she, "let *me* at him," says she, "it's I that's used to
give a man a lickin' every day in the week; you're bowld an the
head now, you vagabone," says she "but if I had you alone," says
she, "no matther if I wouldn't take the consait out o' your—"*New
pittayatees*"—out o' your braggin' heart;" and that's the way she wint
an ballyraggin' him; and, by gor, they all tuk patthern afther her, and
abused him, my dear, to that degree, that I vow to the Lord, the very
dogs in the sthreet wouldn't lick his blood.

SAL.—Oh, my blissin' an thim.

KAT.—And with that, one and all, they begun to cry—"*New
pittayatees!*"—they began to cry him down; and, at last, they all swore
out, "Hell's bell attind your berrin'," says they, "you vagabone," as
they just tuk him up by the scruff o' the neck, and threw him down
the stairs; every step he'd take, you'd think he'd brake his neck,
(Glory be to God!) and so I got rid o' the ruffin; and then they left
me cryin'—"*New pittayatees!*"—cryin' afther the vagabone—though
the angels knows well he wasn't desarvin' o' one precious drop that
fell from my two good-lookin' eyes:—and, oh! but the condition
he left me in.

SAL.—Lord look down an you!

KAT.—And a purty sight it id be, if you could see how I was lyin'
in the middle o' the flure, cryin'—"*New pittayatees!*"—cryin' and
roarin', and the poor child, with his eye knocked out, in the corner,
cryin'—"*New pittayatees!*"—and, indeed, every one in the place was
cryin'—"*New pittayatees!*"—was cryin' murther.

SAL.—And no wondher, Katty dear.

KAT.—Oh, bud that's not all. If you seen the condition the place
was in afther it; it was turned upside down, like a beggar's breeches.
Throth, I'd rather be at a bull-bait than at it—enough to make an
honest woman cry—"*New pittayatees!*"—to see the daycent room
rack'd and ruin'd, and my cap tore aff my head into tatthers—throth,
you might riddle bull-dogs through it; and bad luck to the hap'orth
he left me, but a few—"*New pittayatees!*"—a few coppers; for the
morodin' thief spint all his—"*New pittayatees!*"—all his wages o' the
whole week in makin' a baste iv himself; and God knows but that

comes aisy to him! and divil a thing had I to put inside my face, nor a dhrop to dhrink, barrin' a few—"*New pittayatees!*"—a few grains o' tay, and the ind iv a quarther o' sugar, and my eyes as big as your fist, and as black as the jot (savin' your presence), and a beautiful dish iv—"*New pittayatees!*"—dish iv delf, that I bought only last week in Temple-bar, bruk in three halves, in the middle o' the ruction—and the rint o' the room not ped—and I dipindin' only an—"*New pittayatees*"—an cryin' a sieve-full o' pratees, or schreechin' a lock o' savoys, or the like.

But I'll not brake your heart any more, Sally dear;—God's good, and never opens one door but he shuts another, and that's the way iv it; an' strinthins the wake with—"*New pittayatees*"—with his purtection—and may the widdy and the orphin's blessin' be an his name, I pray!—And my thrust is in Divine Providence, that was always good to me—and sure I don't despair; but not a night that I kneel down to say my prayers, that I don't pray for—"*New pittayatees*"—for all manner o' bad luck to attind that vagabone, Mike M'Evoy. My curse light an him this blessid minit; and—

[*A voice at a distance calls, "Potatoes."*]

KAT.—Who calls?—(*Perceives her customer*)—Here, Ma'am,—Good-bye, Sally, darlint—good-bye. *"New pittay-a-tees."*

[*Exit Katty by the Cross Poddle*]

1.   Getting drunk.
2.   Intoxicated.

Paddy the Sport

"My lord made himself much sport out of him; by his authority he remains here, which he thinks is a patent for his sauciness."

"He will lie, Sir, with such volubility, that you would think truth were a fool.—Drunkenness is his best virtue."

ALL'S WELL THAT ENDS WELL

URING A SOJOURN OF SOME days in the county of ——, visiting a friend, who was anxious to afford as much amusement to his guests as country sports could furnish, "the dog and the gun" were, of course, put into requisition; and the subject of this sketch was a constant attendant on the shooting-party.

He was a tall, loose-made, middle-aged man, rather on the elder side of middle-age, perhaps—fond of wearing an oil-skinned hat and a red waistcoat—much given to lying and tobacco, and an admirable hand at filling a game-bag or emptying a whiskey-flask; and if game was scarce in the stubbles, Paddy was sure to create plenty of another sort for his master's party, by the marvellous stories he had ever at his command. Such was "Paddy the Sport," as the country-people invariably called him.

Paddy was fond of dealing in mystification, which he practised often on the peasants, whom he looked upon as an inferior class of beings to himself—considering that his office of sportsman conferred a rank upon him that placed him considerably above them, to say nothing of the respect that was due to one so adroit in the use of the gun as himself; and, by the way, it was quite a scene to watch the air of self-complacency that Paddy, after letting fly both barrels into a covey, and dropping his brace of birds as dead as a stone, quietly let down the piece from his shoulder, and commenced reloading, looking about him the while with an admirable carelessness, and when his piece was ready for action again, returning his ramrod with the air of a master, and then, throwing the gun into the hollow of his arm, walk forward to the spot where the birds were lying, and pick them up in the most business-like manner.

But to return to Paddy's love of mystification. One day I accompanied him, or perhaps it would be fitter to say he acted as guide, in leading me across a country to a particular point, where I wanted to make a sketch. His dogs and gun, of course, bore him company, though I was only armed with my portfolio; and we beat across the fields, merrily enough, until the day became overcast, and a heavy squall of wind and rain forced us to seek. shelter in the first cottage we arrived at. Here the good woman's apron was employed in an instant in dusting a three-legged stool to offer to "the gintleman," and "Paddy the Sport" was hailed with welcome by every one in the house, with whom he entered into conversation in his usual strain of banter and mystification.

I listened for some time to the passing discourse; but the bad weather still continuing, I began amusing myself, until it should clear, in making an outline of a group of dogs that were stretched upon the floor of the cabin, in a small green sketching-book that I generally carry about me for less important memoranda. This soon caused a profound silence around me; the silence was succeeded by a broken whispering, and Mr Paddy, at last approaching me with a timidity of manner I could not account for said —"Sure, Sir, it wouldn't be worth your while to mind puttin' down the pup?" pointing to the one that had approached the group of dogs, and had commenced his awkward gambols with his seniors.

I told him I considered the pup as the most desirable thing to notice; but scarcely were the words uttered, until the old woman cried out, "Terry, take that cur out o' that—I'm sure I don't know what brings all the dogs here:" and Terry caught up the pup in his arms, and was running away with him, when I called after him to stop; but 'twas in vain. He ran like a hare from me; and the old lady, seizing a branch of a furze-bush from a heap of them that were stowed beside the chimney corner for fuel, made an onset on the dogs, and drove them yelping from the house.

I was astonished at this, and perceived that the air of every one in the cottage was altered towards me; and, instead of the civility which had saluted my entrance, estranged looks, or direct ones of no friendly character, were too evident. I was about to inquire the cause, when Paddy the Sport, going to the door, and casting a weather-wise look abroad, said, "I think, Sir, we may as well be goin'—and, indeed, the day's clearin' up fine afther all, and 'ill be beautiful yit. Good-bye to you, Mrs Flannerty,"—and off went Paddy; and I followed immediately, having expressed my thanks to the aforesaid Mrs Flannerty, making my most engaging adieu, which, however, was scarcely returned.

On coming up with my conductor, I questioned him touching what the cause might be of the strange alteration in the manner of the cottagers, but all his answers were unsatisfactory or evasive.

We pursued our course to the point of destination. The day cleared, as was prophesied—Paddy killed his game—I made my sketch—and we bent our course homeward, as the evening was closing. After proceeding for a mile or two, I pointed to a tree in the distance, and asked Paddy what very large bird it could be that as sitting in it.

After looking harply for some time, he said, "It's a bird, is it— throth, it's a bird that never flew yit."

"What is it then?" said I.

"It's a dog that's hangin'," said he.

And he was right—for as we approached, it became more evident every moment. But my surprise was excited, when having scarcely passed the suspended dog, another tree rose up in my view, in advance, decorated by a pendant brace of the same breed.

"By the powers! there's two more o' thim," shouted Paddy. "Why, at this rate, they've had more sportin' nor myself," said he. And I could see an expression of mischievous delight playing over the features of Mr Paddy, as he uttered the sentence.

As we proceeded, we perceived almost every second bush had been converted into a gallows for the canine race; and I could not help remarking to my companion, that we were certainly in a very hang-dog country.

"Throth, thin, you may thank yourself for it," said he, laughing outright; for up to this period, his mirth, though increasing at every fresh execution perceived, had been smothered.

"Thank myself!" said I—"how?"

"By my sowl, you frekened the whole country this mornin'," said he, "with that little green book o' yours—"

"Is it my sketch-book?" said I.

"By gor, all the people thought it was a *ketch*-book, sure enough, and that you wor goin' round the counthry, to ketch all the dogs in it, and make thim pay—"

"What do you mean?" said I.

"Is it what I mane you want to know, sir?— throth, thin, I don't know how I can tell it to a gintleman, at all at all."

"Oh, you may tell me."

"By gor, Sir, I wouldn't like offindin' your honour; but you see (since you must know, sir), that whin *you tuk* that little green book out iv your pocket, *they tuk* you for—savin' your presence—by gor, I don't like tellin' you."

"Tut, nonsense, man," said I.

"Well, sir (since you *must* know), by dad, they tuk you—I beg your honour's pardon—but, by dad, they tuk you for a tax-gatherer."

"A tax-gatherer!"

"Divil a lie in it; and whin they seen you takin' off the dogs, they thought it was to count thim, for to make thim pay for thim; and so, by dad, they thought it best, I suppose, to hang them out o' the way."

"Ha! Paddy," said I, "I see this is a piece of your knavery, to bewilder the poor people."

"Is it me?" says Paddy, with a look of assumed innocence, that avowed, in the most provoking manner, the inward triumph of Paddy in his own hoax.

"'Twas too much, Paddy," said I, "to practise so far on innocent people."

"Innocent!" said Paddy. "They're just about as innocent as coal o' fire in a bag o' flax."

"And the poor animals, too!" said I.

"Is it the blackguard curs?" said Paddy, in the most sportsmalike wonder at my commiserating any but a spaniel or pointer.

"Throth, thin, sir, to tell you thruth, I let thim go an in their mistake, and I seen all along how't would be, and, 'pon my conscience, but a happy riddance the counthry will have o' sich riff-raff varmint of cabin curs. Why, sir, the mangy mongrels goes about airly in the sayson, moroding through the corn, and murthers the young birds, and does not let them come to their full time, to be killed in their nath'ral way, and ruinin' gintlemen's sport into the bargain and sure hangin' is all that's good for them."

So much for Paddy's mystifying powers. Of this coup he was not a little vain, and many a laugh he has made at my expense afterwards, by telling the story of the "painter gintleman that was mistuk for a tax-gatherer."

Paddy being a professed story-teller, and a notorious liar, it may be naturally inferred that he dealt largely in fairy tales and ghost stories. Talking of fairies one day, for the purpose of exciting him to say something of them, I inquired if there were many fairies in that part of the country?

"Ah! no, sir!" said be, with the air of a sorrowing patriot—"not now. There was wanst a power of fairies used to keep about the place; but sence the *rale* quol'ty—the good ould families—has left it, and the upstarts has kem into it—the fairies has quitted it all out, and wouldn't stay here, but is gone farther back into Connaught, where the ould blood is."

"But, I dare say, you have seen them sometimes?"

"No, indeed, sir. I never saw thim, barrin' wanst, and that was whin I was a boy; but I heerd them often."

"How did you know it was fairies you heard?"

"Oh, what else could it be? Sure it was crossin' out over a road I was in the time o' the ruction, and heard full a thousand men marchin' down the road, and by dad I lay down in the gripe o' the ditch, not wishin' to be seen, nor liken to be throublesome to thim; and I watched who they wor, and was peepin' out iv a turf o' rishes, when what should I see but nothin' at all, to all appearance, but the thrampin' o' min, and a clashin', and a jinglin', that you'd think the infanthry, and yeomanthry, and cavalthry was in it, and not a sight iv anthing to be seen, but the brightest o' moonlight that ever kem out o' the hivins."

"And that was all?"

"Divil a more; and by dad 'twas more nor I'd like to see or to hear agin."

"But you never absolutely saw any fairies?"

"Why, indeed, sir, to say that I seen thim, that is with my own eyes, wouldn't be thrue, barrin' wanst, as I said before, and that's many a long day ago, whin I was a boy, and I and another chap was watchin' turf in a bog; and whin the night was fallin' and we wor goin' home, 'What would you think,' says I, 'Charley, if we wor to go home by old Shaughnessey's field, and stale a shafe o' pays?' So he agreed, and off we wint to stale the pays; but whin we got over the fince, and was creepin' along the furrows for fear of bein' seen, I heerd some one runnin' afther me, and I thought we wor cotch, myself and the boy, and I turned round, and with that I seen two girls dhressed in white—throth I never seen sitch white in my born days—they wor as white as the blown snow, and runnin' like the wind, and I knew at wanst that they wor fairies, and I threw myself down an my face, and by dad I was afeard to look up for nigh half an hour."

I inquired of him what sort of faces these fine girls had.

"Oh, the divil a stim o' their faytures I could see; for the minit I clapt my eyes an thim, knowin' they wor fairies, I fell down, and darn't look at them twicet."

"It was a pity you did not remark them," said I.

"And do you think it's a fool I am, to look twicet at a fairy, and maybe have my eyes whipt out iv my head, or turned into stones, or stone blind, which is all as one."

"Then you can scarcely say you saw them?" says I.

"Oh, by dad, I can say I seen thim, and sware it for that matther; at laste, there was somethin' I seen as white as the blown snow."

"Maybe they were ghosts, and not fairies," said I; "ghosts, they say, are always seen in white."

"Oh, by all that's good, they warn't ghosts, and that I know full well, for I know the differ betune ghosts and fairies."

"You have had experience then in both, I suppose."

"Faix you may say that. Oh I had a wondherful great *appearance* wanst that kem to me, or at laste to the house where I was, for, to be sure, it wasn't to me it kem, why should it? But it was whin I was livin' at the lord's in the next county, before I kem to live with his honour here, that I saw the appearance."

"In what shape did it come?"

"Throth thin I can't well tell you what shape; for you see whin I see it comin' I put my head undher the clothes, and never looked up, nor opened my eyes until I heerd it was gone."

"But how do you know that it was a ghost?"

"Oh, sure all the counthry knew the house was throubled, and, in that was the rayson I had for lavin' it, for when my lord turned me off, he was expectin' that I'd ax to be tuk back agin, and faith sorry he was, I go bail, that I didn't, but I wouldn't stay in the place and it hanted!"

"Then it *was* haunted?"

"To be sure it was; sure I tell you, sir, the sper't kem to me."

"Well, Paddy, that was only civil—returning a visit; for I know you are fond of going to the spirits occasionally."

"Musha, bud your honour is always jokin' me about the dhrop. Oh, bud faith the sper't kem to me, and whin I hid my head undther the clothes, sure didn't I feel the sper't sthrivin' to pull them aff o' me. But wait and I'll tell you how it was. You see, myself and another sarvant was sleepin' in one room, and by the same token, a thievin' rogue he was the same sarvant, and I heerd a step comin' down the stairs, and they wor stone stairs, and the latch was riz, but the door was locked, for I turned the key in it myself; and when the sper't seen the latch was fast, by dad the key was turned in the door (though it was inside, av coorse), and the sper't walked in, and I heerd the appearance walkin' about the place, and it kem and shuk me: but, as I tould you, I shut my eyes, and rowled my head up in the clothes; well with that, it went and raked the fire (for I suppose it was cowld), but the fire was a'most gone out, and with that it went to the turf-bucket to see if there was any sods there to throw an the fire; but not a sod there was left, for we wor sittin' up late indeed (it bein' the young lord's birthday, and we wor drinkin' his health), and when it couldn't find any turf in the bucket, bad cess to me but it began to kick the buckets up and down the room for spite, and divil sich a clatter I ever heerd as the sper't made, kickin' the turf-bucket like a fut-ball round the place; and whin it was tired plazin' itself that-a-way, the appearance came and shuk me agin, and I roared and bawled at last, and thin away it went, and slammed the door afther it, that you'd think it id pull the house down."

"I'm afraid, Paddy," said I, "that this was nothing more than a troublesome dream."

"Is it a dhrame your honour! That a dhrame! By my sowl, that id be a quare dhrame! Oh, in throth it was no dhrame it was, but an appearance; but indeed, afther, I often thought it was an appearance for death, for the young lord never lived to see another birth-day. Oh, you may look at me, sir, but it's truth. Aye, and I'll tell you what's more: the young lord, the last time I seen him out, was one day he was huntin' and he came in from the stables, through the back yard, and passed through that very room to go up by the back stairs, and, as he wint in through that very door that the appearance slammed afther it—what would you think, but he slammed the door afther hin the very same way; and indeed I thrimbled when I thought iv it. He was in a hurry to be sure but I think there was some maynin' in it"—Paddy looked mysterious.

After the foregoing satisfactory manner in which Paddy showed so clearly that he understood the difference between a ghost and a fairy, he proceeded to enlighten me with the further distinction of a spirit, from either of them. This was so very abstruse, that I shall not attempt to take the elucidation of the point out of Paddy's own hands; and should you, gentle reader, ever have the good fortune to make his acquaintance, Paddy, I have no doubt, will clear up the matter as fully and clearly to your satisfaction as he did to mine. But I must allow Paddy to proceed in his own way.

"Well, sir, before I go an to show you the differ betune the fairies and sper'ts, I must tell you about a mighty quare thrick the fairies was goin' to play at the lord's house, where the appearance kem to me, only that the nurse (and she was an aunt o' my own) had the good luck to baulk thim. You see the way it was, was this. The child was a man-child, and it was the first boy was in the family for many a long day; for they say there was a prophecy standin' agin the family, that there should be no son to inherit but at last there was a boy, and a lovely fine babby it was, as you'd see in a summer's day; and so, one evenin', that the fam'ly, my lord and my lady, and all o' thim, was gone out, and gev the nurse all sorts o' charges about takin' care o' the child, she was not long alone, whin the housekeeper kem to her, and ax'd her to come down stairs; where she had a party; and they expected to be mighty pleasant, and was to have great goins an; and so the nurse said she didn't like lavin the child, and all to that; but, howsomever, she was beguiled into the thing; and she said at last that as soon as she left the child out iv her lap, where she was hushing it to sleep, foreninst the fire, that she'd go down to the rest o' the sarvants, and take share o' what was goin'.

"Well, at last the child was fast asleep, and the nurse laid it an the bed, as careful as if it was goolden diamonds, and tucked the curtains roun' about the bed, and made it as safe as Newgate, and thin she wint down, and joined the divarshin—and merry enough they wor, at playin' iv cards, and dhrinkin' punch, and dancin', and the like o' that.

"But I must tell you, that before she wint down at all, she left one o' the housemaids to stay in the room, and charged her, on her apparel, not to lave the place until she kem back; but, for all that, her fears wouldn't let he be aisy; and, indeed, it was powerful lucky that she had an inklin' o' what was goin' an. For, what id you think, but the blackguard iv a housemaid, as soon as she gets the nurse's back turned, she ups and she goes to another party that was in the sarvants' hall, wid the undher-sarvants; for whin the lord's back was turned, you see, the house was all as one as a play-house, fairly turned upside down.

"Well, as I said, the nurse (undher God) had an inklin' o' what was to be: for, though there was all sorts o' divarshin goin' an in the housekeeper's room, she could not keep the child out iv her head, and she thought she heerd the screeches av it ringin' in her ear every minit, although she knew full well she was far beyant where the cry o' the child could be heerd—but still the cry was as plain in her ear as the ear-ring she had in it; and so at last she grewn so onaisy about the child, that she was goin' up stairs agin—but she was stopped by one, and another coaxed her, and another laughed at her, till at last she grew ashamed of doin' what was right (and God knows, but many a one iv uz is laughed out o' doin' a right thing), and so she sat down agin—but the cry in her ears wouldn't let her be aisy; and at last she tuk up her candle, and away she wint up stairs.

"Well, afther passin' the two first flights, sure enough she heerd the child a screechin', that id go to your heart; and with that she hurried up so fast, that the candle a'most wint out with the draught; and she run into the room, and wint up to the bed, callin' out *My lanna bawn*, and all to that, to soother the child; and pullin' open the bed-curtain, to take the darlin' up—but what would you think, not a sign o' the child was in the bed, good, bad, or indifferent; and she thonght the life id lave her; for thin she was afeard the child dhropped out o' the bed—though she thought the curtains was tucked so fast and so close, that no accident could happen; and so she run round to the other side, to take up the child (though, indeed, she was afeard she'd see it with its brains dashed out), and lo and behould you, divil a taste

av it was there, though she heerd it screechin' as if it was murtherin':
and so thin she didn't know what in the wide world to do; and she
run rootin' into every corner o' the room, lookin' for it; but bad cess
to the child she could find—whin all iv a suddint, turnin' her eyes
to the bed agin, what did she persave, but the fut-carpet that wint
round the bed, goin' by little and little undher it, as if some one was
pullin' it; and so she made a dart at the carpet, and cotch hould o'
the ind iv it—and, with that, what should she see, but the baby lyin'
in the middle o' the fat-carpet, as if it was dhrawin' down into the
flure, undher the bed; one half o' the babby was out o' sight already,
undher the boords, whin the nurse seen it, and it screechin' like a
sae-gull, and she laid houl' iv it; and, faith, she often towl' myself, that
she was obleeged to give a good sthrong pull before she could get
the child from the fairies—"

"Then it was the fairies were taking the child away?" said I.

"Who else would it be?" said Paddy! "Sure the carpet wouldn't
be runnin' undher the bed itself, if it wasn't pulled by the fairies!
—besides, I towl' you there was a prophecy stannin' agin the male
boys of the lord's fam'ly."

"I hope, however, *that* boy lived?"

"Oh yes, sir, the charm was bruk that night; for the other childher
used be tuk away always by the fairies; and that night the child id
have been tuk, only for the nurse, that was givin (undher God) to
undherstan' the screechin' in her ears, and arrived betimes to ketch
howl o' the carpet; and baulk the fairies; for all knowledgable people
I ever heerd, says, that if you baulk the fairies *wanst*, they'll lave you
alone evermore."

"Pray, did she *see* any of the fairies that were stealing the child?"

"No, sir; the fairies doesn't love to be seen, and seldom at all you
get a sight iv them; and that's the differ I was speakin' iv to you
betune fairies and sper'ts. Now the sper'ts is always seen in some
shape or other; and maybe it id be a bird, or a shafe o' corn, or a big
stone, or a hape o' dune, or the like a' that, and never know 'twas a
sper't at all, antil you wor made sinsible av it, some how or other;
maybe it id be that you wor comin' home from a friend's house late

at night, and you might fall down, and couldn't keep a leg undher you, and not know why, barrin' it was a sper't misled you—and maybe it's in a ditch you'd find yourself asleep in the mornin' when you woke."

"I dare say, Paddy, that same has happened to yourself before now?"

"Throth, and you may say that, sir; but the commonest thing in life is for a sper't for to take the shape iv a dog—which is a favourite shape with sper't—and, indeed, Tim Mooney, the miller, in the next town, was a'most frekened out iv his life by a sper't that-a-way; and he'd ha' been murthered, only he had the good bock to have a *rale* dog wid him—and a rale dog is he finest thing in the world agin sper'ts."

"How do you account for that, Paddy?"

"Bekase, sir, the dog's the most sinsible, and the bowldest baste, barrin' the cock, which is bowldher for his size than any o' God's craythurs; and so, whin the cock crows, all evil sper'ts vanishes; and the dog bein', as I said, bowld, and sinsible also, is mighty good; bekides, you couldn't make a cock your companion, it wouldn't be nath'ral to rayson, you know—and therefore a dog is the finest thing in the world for a man to have with him in throublesome places: but I must tell you, that though sper'ts dhreads a dog, a fairy doesn't mind him—for I have heerd o' fairies ridin' a dog, all as one as a monkey—and a lanthern also is good, for the sper't o' darkness dhreads the light. But this is not tellin' you about Mooney the miller:—he was comin' home, you see, from a neighbour's, and had to pass by a rath; and when he just kem to the rath, his dog that was wid him (and a brave dog he was, by the same token) began to growl, an gev a low bark; and with that, the miller seen a great big baste of a black dog comin' up to thim, and walks a one side av him, all as one as if he was his masther; with that Mooney's own dog growled agin, and runs betune his master's legs, and there he staid walkin' on wid him, for to purtect him; and the miller was frekened a'most out iv his life, and his hair stood up sthrait an his head, that he was obleeged to put his hand up to his hat, and shove it down

an his head, and three times it was that way, that his hair was risin'
the hat aff his head with the fright, and he was obleeged to howld
it down, and his dog growlin' all the time, and the black thief iv a
dog keepin' dodgin' him along, and his eyes like coals o' fire, and the
terriblest smell of sulphur, I hear, that could be, all the time, till at
last they came to a little sthrame that di'cided the road; and there, my
dear, the sper't disappeared, not bein' able to pass runnin' wather; for
sper'ts, sir, is always waken'd with wather."

"That I believe," said I; "but, I think, Paddy, you seldom put spirits
to so severe a trial."

"Ah thin, but your honour will you never give over jeerin' me
about the dhrop. But, in throth, what I'm tellin' you is thrue about
it—runnin' wather desthroys sper'ts."

"Indeed, Paddy, I know that is your opinion."

"Oh! murther, murther!—there I made a slip agin, and never seen
it till your honour had the advantage o' me. Well, no matther, it's
good any way; but, indeed, I think it has so good a good name iv its
own that it's a pity to spile it, baptism' it any more."

Such were the marvellous yarns that Paddy was constantly
spinning. Indeed he had a pride, I rather think, in being considered
equally expert at "the long bow" as at the rifle; and if he had not
a bouncer to astonish his hearers with, he endeavoured that his
ordinary strain of conversation, or his answer to the commonest
question, should be of a nature to surprise them. Such was his reply
one morning to his master, when he asked Paddy what was the cause
of his being so hoarse.

"Indeed, sir," answered Paddy, "it's a cowld I got, and indeed myself
doesn't know how I cotch cowld, barrin' that I slep' in a field last
night, and forgot to shut the gate afther me."

"Ah, Paddy," said the squire, "the old story—you were drunk as
usual, and couldn't find your way home. You're a shocking fellow,
and you'll never get on, as long as you give yourself up to whiskey."

"Why thin, your honour, sure that's the rayson I ought to get an
the fasther for isn't a 'spur in the head worth two in the heel,' as the
ould sayin' is?"

Here a laugh from the squire's guests turned the scale in Paddy favour.

"I give you up, Paddy," said the roaster—"you're a sad dog—worse than Larry Lanigan."

"Oh, murther! Is it Lanigan you'd be afther comparin' me to," said Paddy. "Why, Lanigan is the complatest dhrinker in Ireland—by my sowkins—more whiskey goes through Lanigan than any other *worm* in the county. Is it Lanigan? Faiks, that's the lad could take the consait out iv a gallon o' sper'ts, without quittin' it. Throth, Lanigan is just the very chap that id go to first mass every mornin' in the year, if holy wather was whiskey."

This last reply left Paddy in possession of the field, and no further attack was made upon him on the score of his love of "the dhrop!" and this triumph on his part excited him to exert himself in creating mirth for the gentlemen who formed the shooting party. One of the company retailed that well-known joke made by Lord Norbury, viz, when a certain gentleman declared that he had shot twenty hares before breakfast, his lordship replied, that he *must have fired at a wig.*

Here Paddy declared that he thought "it was no great shootin'" to kill twenty hares, for that he had shot seventy-five brace of rabbits in one day.

"Seventy-five brace!" was laughed forth from every one present.

"Bad loock to the lie in it," said Paddy.

"Oh, be easy, Paddy," said his master.

"There it is now; and you won't b'live me? Why thin, in throth it's not that I'm proud iv it, I tell you, for I don't think it was any great things iv shootin' at all at all."

Here a louder burst of merriment than the former hailed Paddy's declaration.

"Well now," said Paddy, "if yiz be quiet, and listen to me, I'll explain it to your satisfaction. You see, it was in one iv the islans aff the shore there," and he pointed seawards—"it was in one o' the far islans out there where rabbits are so plinty, and runnin' so thick that you can scarcely see the grass."

"Because the island is all sand," said his master.

"No, indeed now!—though you thought you had me there," said Paddy, very quietly. "It's not the sandy islan, at all, bud one farther out."

"Which of them?"

"Do you know, the little one with the black rock?"

"Yes."

"Well it's not that. But you know—"

"Arrah! Can't you tell his honour," said a peasant who was an attendant on the party, to carry the game—"can't you tell his honour at wanst, and not be delayin'—"

Paddy turned on this plebeian intruder with the coolest contempt, and said, "Hurry no man's cattle, get a jackass for yourself—" and then resumed—"Well, sir, bud you know the island with the sharp headlan'—"

"Yes."

"Well, it's not that either; but if you—"

"At this rate, Paddy," said the Squire, "we shall never hear which island this wonderful rabbit burrow is in. How would you steer for it after passing Innismoyle?"

"Why, thin, you should steer about nor-west, and when you cleared the black rocks you'd have the sandy islan bearin' over your larboard bow, and thin you'd see the islan I spake av, when you run about as far as—"

"Pooh! pooh!" said the squire, "you're dreaming, Paddy; there's no such island at all."

"By my sowl, there is, beggin' your honour's pardon."

"It's very odd I never saw it."

"Indeed it's a wondher, sure enough."

"Oh! it can't be," said the squire. "How big is it?"

"Oh! by dad, it's as big as ever it'll be," said Paddy, chuckling.

This answer turned the laugh against the squire again, who gave up further cross-questioning of Paddy, whose readiness of converting his answers into jokes generally frustrated any querist who was hardy enough to engage with Paddy in the hope of puzzling him.

"Paddy," said the squire, "after that wonderful rabbit adventure perhaps you would favour the gentlemen with that story you told me once, about a fox?"

Indeed and I will, plaze your honor," said Paddy, "though I know full well the divil a one word iv it you b'live, nor the gintlemen won't either, though you're axin' me for it—but only want to laugh at me, and call me a big liar, whin my back's turned."

"Maybe we wouldn't wait for your back being turned, Paddy, to honour you with that title."

"Oh, indeed, I'm not sayin' you wouldn't do it as soon foreninst my face, your honour, as you often did before, and will agin, plaze God, and welkim—"

"Well, Paddy, say no more about that, but let's have the story."

"Sure I'm losin' no time, only tellin' the gintlemen beforehand, that it's what they'll be callin' it, a lie—and indeed it's uncommon, sure enough; but you see, gintlemen, you must remember that the fox is the cunnin'est baste in the world, barrin' the wran—"

Here Paddy was questioned why he considered the wren as cunnin a *baste* as the fox.

"Why, sir, bekase all birds build their nest wid one hole to it only, excep'n the wran; but the wran builds two holes to the nest, and so that if any inimy comes to disturb it upon one door, it can go out an the other. But the fox is 'cute to that degree, that there's many mortial a fool to him—and, by dad, the fox could buy and sell many a Christian, as you'll soon see by-and-by, when I tell you what happened to a wood-ranger that I knew wanst, and a dacent man he was, and wouldn't say the thing in a lie.

"Well, you see, he kem home one night, mighty tired—for he was out wid a party in the domain, cock-shootin' that day; and whin he got back to his lodge, he threw a few logs o' wood an the fire, to make himself comfortable, an he tuk whatever little matther he had for his supper; and, afther that, he felt himself so tired, that he wint to bed. But you're to understhan' that, though he wint to bed, it was more for to rest himself like, than to sleep, for it was airly; and so he jist went into bed, and there he divarted himself lookin' at the fire, that was blazin' as merry as a bonfire an the hearth.

"Well, as he was lyin' that-a-way, jist thinkin' o' nothin' at all, what should come into the place but a fox. But I must tell you, what I forgot to tell you before, that the ranger's house was on the bordhers o' the wood, and he had no one to live wid him but himself, barrin' the dogs that he had the care iv, that was his only companions, and he had a hole cut an the door, with a swingin' boord to it, that the dogs might go in or out accordin' as it plazed thim; and, by dad, the fox came in, as I tould you, through the hole in the door, as bould as a ram, and walked over to the fire, and sat down foreninst it.

"Now, it was mighty provokin' that all the dogs was out—they wor rovin' about the wood, you see, lookin' for to catch rabbits to ate, or some other mischief, and so it happened that there wasn't as much as one individual dog in the place; and, by gor, I'll go bail the fox knew that right well, before he put his nose inside the ranger's lodge.

"Well, the ranger was in hopes some o' the dogs id come home and ketch the chap, and he was loath to stir hand or fut himself, afeard o'freghtenin' away the fox; but, by gor, he could hardly keep his timper at all at all, when he seen the fox take his pipe off o' the hob, where he left it afore he wint to bed, and puttin' the bowl o' the pipe into the fire to kindle it (it's as thrue as I'm here), he began to smoke foreninst the fire, as nath'ral as any other man you ever seen.

"'Musha, bad luck to your impidence, you long-tailed blaguard,' says the ranger, 'and is it smokin' my pipe you are? Oh, thin, by this and by that, if I had my gun convaynient to me, it's fire and smoke of another sort, and what you wouldn't bargain for, I'd give you,' says he. But still he was loath to stir, hopin' the dogs id come home; and, 'by gor, my fine fellow,' says he to the fox, 'if one o' the dogs comes home, salpethre wouldn't save you, and that's a sthrong pickle.'

"So, with that, he watched antil the fox wasn't mindin' him, but was busy shakin' the cindhers out o' the pipe, whin he was done wid it, and so the ranger thought he was goin' to go immediately afther gitten' an air o' the fire and a shough o' the pipe; and so, says he, 'Faiks, my lad, I won't let you go so aisy as all that, as cunnin' as you think yourself;' and with that he made a dart out o' bed, and run over to the door, and got betune it and the fox; and 'now,' says he, 'your bread's baked, my buck, and maybe my lord won't have a fine run out o' you, and the dogs at your brush every yard, you morodin' theif, and the divil mind you,' says he, 'for your impidence—for sure, if you hadn't the impidence of a highwayman's horse, it's not into my very house, undher my nose, yu'd daar for to come;' and with that, he began to whistle for the dogs; and the fox, that stood eyin' him all the time while he was spakin', began to think it was time to be joggin' whin he heard the whistle and says the fox to himself, 'Throth, indeed, you think yourself a mighty great ranger now,' says he, 'and you think you're very cute, but upon my tail, and that's a big oath, I'd be long sorry to let sitch a mallet-headed bog-throtter as yourself take a advantage o' me, and I'll engage,' says the fox, 'I'll make you lave the door soon and suddint;' and with that, he turned to where the ranger's brogues was lyin' hard by beside the fire, and, what would you think, but the fox tuk up one o' the brogues, and wint over to the fire and threw it into it.

"'I think that'll make you start,' says the fox.

"'Divil resave the start,' says the ranger—'that won't do, my buck,' says he; 'the brogue may burn to cindhers,' says he, 'but out o' this I won't stir;' and thin, puttin' his fingers into his mouth, he gev a blast iv a whistle you'd hear a mile off, and shouted for the dogs.

"'So that won't do,' says the fox. 'Well, I must thry another offer,' says he; and, with that, he tuk up the other brogue and threw it into the fire too.

"'There, now,' says he, 'you may keep the other company,' says he; and there's a pair o' ye now, as the divil said to his knee-buckles.'

"'Oh, you thievin' varmint,' says the ranger, 'you won't lave me a tack to my feet; but no matther,' says he, 'your head's worth more nor a pair o' brogues to me, any day;' and, by the Piper o' Blessintown, you're money in my pocket this minit,' says he; and with that, the finger was in his mouth agin, and he was goin' to whistle, whin, what would you think, but up sits the fox an his hunkers, and puts his two forepaws into his mouth, makin' game o' the ranger—(bad luck to the lie I tell you).

"Well, the ranger, and no wondher, although in a rage he was, couldn't help laughin' at the thought o' the fox mockin' him, and, by dad, he tuk sitch a fit o' laughin', that he couldn't whistle, and that was the 'cuteness o' the fox to gain time; but whin his first laugh was over, the ranger recovered himself, and gev another whistle; and so says the fox, 'By my sowl,' says he, 'I think it wouldn't be good for my health to stay here much longer, and I mustn't be thriflin' with that blackguard ranger any more,' says he, 'and I must make him sinsible that it is time to let me go; and though he hasn't understan'in' to be sorry for his brogues, I'll go bail I'll make him lave that,' says he, 'before he'd say *sparables*'—and, with that, what do you think the fox done? By all that's good—and the ranger himself towld me out iv his own mouth, and said he would never have b'lieved it, only he seen it—the fox tuk a lighted piece iv a log out o' the blazin' fire, and run over wid it to the ranger's bed, and was goin' to throw it into the sthraw, and burn him out of house and home; so when the ranger seen that, he gev a shout out iv him—

"'Hilloo! hilloo! you murdherhin' villian,' says he, 'you're worse nor Captain Rock; is it goin' to burn me out you are, you red rogue iv a Ribbonman?' and he made a dart betune him and the bed, to save the house from bein' burned; but, my jew'l, that was all the fox wanted—and as soon as the ranger quitted the hole in the door that he was standin' foreninst, the fox let go the blazin' faggit, and made one jump through the door, and escaped.

"But before he wint, the ranger gev me his oath, that the fox turned round and gev him the most contemptible look he ever got in his life, and showed every tooth in his head with laughin'; and at last he put out his tongue at him, as much as to say—'You've missed me, like your mammy's blessin',' and off wid him!—like a flesh o' lightenin'."

National Minstrelsy

Ballads and Ballad Singers

Give me the making of a people's *ballads*, and let who will enact their laws.—*Fletcher of Saltoun*

Valdius oblectat populum, meliusque moratur,
Quam versus inopes rerum, negaeque canoae. *Hor. A. P.*

I T IS WELL REMARKED BY Mr Addison, in his justly celebrated paper on the ballad of "The Children in the Wood," of which Mr Godwin has lately given us so admirable an amplification in his novel of "Cloudesley," that "those only who are endowed with true greatness of soul and genius can divest themselves of the little images of ridicule, and admire nature in her simplicity and nakedness" of beauty. We trust, therefore, that we shall not only be forgiven but commended by our most thinking public, for the zeal and diligence with which we have, according to the Horatian precept, devoted sleepless nights and days to the recovery of some of those precious gems of taste and genius, which adorn what may, in the strictest sense, be termed "our national literature," and which, according to

the notion of the grave Scotch politician quoted above, moves and
influences the people,

> And wields at will the fierce democracy,

more than any other species of writing whatever.

Notwithstanding the laborious researches of our countryman,
Mr Edward Bunting, and the elegant adaptations of Mr Moore, we
confess that we indulge in a pleasing belief, that now, for the first
time, most of the reliques which will be found embalmed in the
following paper, are rescued from the chilling gripe of forgetfulness,
and reserved as a κτημα ες αει—a possession for ever, to the envy of
surrounding nations, and the admiration of the world.

Your ballad singer, let us tell you, is a person of no despicable
renown, whatever you, reader, gentle or simple, may think—ay, or
say to the contrary. It may be that you rejoice in possessing the
luxury of a carriage, and so—rolling along our metropolitan world,
escaping the jar and jostle of us wayfaring pedestrians, by the
sliding smoothness of patent axles and Macadam—*you* have heard
but the distant murmur of the ballad strain, and asked, perhaps in a
wondering tone,—

What means that faint halloo?

Or, haply, you are an equestrian exquisite, and your charger has taken fright at the admiring auditory thronging round the minstrel, and spared your fashionable ears nearly at the expense of your still more fashionable neck, starched into the newest stiffness; or you may chance to be a dandy of inferior grade, and only ride that homely yet handy animal, yclept in the vulgar tongue, *shanks's mare*, and are forced to be contented with the "bare ground," consoling yourself for this contact with mere citizens, by staring every woman you meet out of countenance, and preserving yourself from the tainted atmosphere of the dross of humanity that surrounds you by the purifying influence of a cigar. To each and all of you, then, we confidently affirm, that you are not prepared to give any opinion on the subject; and we enjoin you, therefore, to a sacred silence, while we sing, "strains never heard before" to the merry and hearty. You may, if you like it, go on reading this article, and enlighten your benighted understandings, or turn over to the next, and remain in your "fat contented ignorance" of the sublimity and beauty of our national minstrelsy.

Your ballad-monger is of great antiquity. Homer himself,—

> The blind old man of Scio's rocky shore,
> The father of soul-moving poesy—

sat by the way side, or roved from town to town, and sang

> His own bright rhapsodies.

But if this be going too far back, and you are inclined to tax us with affectation for so classical an authority for Bartle Corcoran's vocation, we shall jump over a handful of centuries, and bring you down "at one fell swoop" to the middle ages, citing the troubadours and jongleurs as examples of the ballad-monger's craft. To be sure, all sentimental young ladies will cry shame upon us at this, and think

of L.E.L. and the Improvisatrice, and remember the fatal fame of
Raoul de Couci. But, gentle young ladies, start not—our ballad-
singers are the true descendants of those worthies, the troubadours;
something the worse for the wear perhaps, just the least in the world
degenerated or so, like many another romantic thing of the same
day.

For instance, your gentle page of *fayre ladye* is, in modern times,
a pert servant-boy, with a snub nose, vying in brilliancy with the
scarlet collar that overflaps his blue jacket. Your faithful bower-
woman has rather a poor representative in the roguish *petite maîtresse*
of a French maid, who is, for all the world, like a milliner' doll,
except in the article of silence. Your gallant knight himself no longer
bestrides a proudly-prancing war-horse, sheathed "in complete
steel," with spear in rest, ready to "answer all comers" in the lists, at
the behest of his ladye love.—No.—Your warrior, now-a-days, is no
longer a "gintleman in the tin clothes," as Jerry Sullivan describes
him, but a very spruce person, in superfine scarlet, ready to answer
all—invitations to dinner. Your warder, or warden, is, in fact, now a
mere hall-porter, and the high-sounding "donjon-keep"—nothing
more nor less than Newgate.

And now, having, we think, successfully proved that your ballad-
singer comes from an "ould ancient family", we trust we have
influenced the artistocratic feelings of our reader in his favour; and
hoping for a patient reading, we subject, first asking pardon for
this somewhat lengthy introduction, in which our anxiety for the
reputation of the ancient and respectable craft of ballad-singing has
betrayed us.

When the day begins to wane, and the evening air is fresh (if
anything can ever be fresh in a city), and people are sauntering
along the streets, as if the business of all were over—of all, save the
lamplighter, he, the only active being amongst a world of loungers,
skipping along from lamp to lamp, which one by one "start into
light" with perspective regularity, telling of the flight of the "flaming
minister" up the long street before you—then we say, it is pleasant to
roam along the quays, for instance, and halt at the foot of each bridge,

or branch off into Capel-street or Parliament-street, or proceed further westward to the more vocal neighbourhood of Bridge or Barrack-streets, and listen to the ballad singers of all denominations that, without fail, are labouring in their vocation in these quarters.

Music, they say, sounds sweetest upon water; and hence the reason, we suppose, of the ballad-singer choosing the vicinity of the river for his trade; and, like that other notorious songster, the nightingale, he, too, prefers the evening for his strains. Ballad-singers, to be sure, may be heard at all times of the day, making tuneful the corners of every street in the city, and moving the vocal air "to testify their hidden residence;" but, by the initiated in ballads, they are detected at once for scurvy pretenders. No ballad-singer of any eminence in his or her profession ever appears until the sun is well down; your she ballad-singers, in particular, are all "maids that love the moon;" and indeed the choicest amongst them, like your very fashionable people at a party, do not condescend to favour their friends by their presence until a good while after the others have made their *entrée.*

The amateur in ballads well knows where he may expect to find good entertainment, just as one calculates the sort of party he may expect to meet by the address on the card of invitation. Your amateur, for instance, would no more lose his time in listening to a performance in Merrion-square, than an officer of the guards would go to a rout in Skinner's-row. No, no—Merrion-square is far too genteel for any thing good in the ballad line. But oh! sweet High-street, and Corn-market—Cutpurse-row, too—(by the bye, always leave your watch and sovereigns at home, and carry your *pocket* handkerchief in your hat, when you go a larking in search of ballad minstrelsy)—and so on to Thomas-street. Your desperate explorer, who with a Columbian courage, pants for greater and more western discoveries, will push on to the Cross-poddle (as far as which point we *once* ventured ourselves, and fished for city trout in the Brithogue), double the *cape* of Tailor's close, turn the corner of Elbow-alley, and penetrate the mysteries of Fumbally's lane, rife in the riches of ballad lore, returning to the civilised haunts of men by the purlieus of Patrick's-close, Golden-lane, and so on through

Squeezegut-alley, until he gets into port—that is, Kevin's-port—and there, at the corner of *Cheater's*-lane, it is hard if he don't get an honest hap'orth of ballad. They are generally loving and pathetic in this quarter, Kevin-street, as if the music of the region were, with an antithetical peculiarity, of a different turn from the hard-hearted saint whose name it bears. Saint Kevin-street is endeared to us by many tender recollections, and here it was that the *iron* entered our sole as we listened, for the first time, to the following touching effusion:—

> Oh J*i*mm*i*-a Jim-my I l*O*ve you well,
> i Love *y*ou be*tt*her nor my tongu*E* Can tell-
> *I* love you well but I da*r* not show it.
> I lo*V*e you well *b*ut let *n*o one kNo*w* it.

What a beautiful union of affection and delicacy in the last line!—the generous confidence of a devoted heart, with the tender timidity of the blushing maid, shrinking at the thought of the discovery of her passion to the multitude: with the sincerity of a Juliet, she openly avows her flame—

> I love you well;

but at the same time wishing to be, as Moore says,

> —Curtain'd from the sight
> Of the gross world,

she cautiously adds,

> But let no one know it.

This is, perhaps, an inferior specimen of the amatory ballad, but as it is one of the early impressions made on our young imaginations, we hope we may be pardoned for giving it place even before those of loftier pretensions:—

Ou revient toujours
  A ses premiers amours.

   The ballad, though coming generally under the denomination of lyric poetry, may be classified under various heads. First in order due, we class the amatory; then there are the political and the polemical; though, indeed, we should follow, we are inclined to think, the order adopted in the favourite corporation phrase of "church and state," and so we shall arrange our ballads more fitly by giving the polemicals the *pas*; the order will then stand thus:—

AMATORY,
POLEMICAL,
PATRIOTIC,
BACCHANALIAN,
DESCRIPTIVE,
POLITICAL,
and
NON-DESCRIPTIVE.

   Sometimes, in the AMATORY, the bewitching blandishments of the fair are portrayed with a force and vivid simplicity which Catallus might envy; thus, in depicting the "taking ways," of Miss Judith O'Reilly, who had, it would seem, a penchant for leading soft-hearted youths "the other way," as Mr Moore delicately expresses it, the minstrel describes the progress of the potent spell:—

Och Judy Riley you use me viley,
And like a child me do coax and decoy,
Its myself thats thinkin while you do be winkin
So soft upon me, you will my heart destroy.

   Again, the poet often revels in the contemplation of the joint attractions of his mistress's beauties and accomplishments; and at the

same time that he tells you she is

> As lovely as Diania,

he exults in announcing that

> She plays on the piania.

While in the description of a *rurial swain* by his innamorata, we are informed that

> Apollo's Gool*d*in hair with his could not compare
> Astonished were All the bebo*u*lders.

Sometimes our ballad bards become enamoured of the simple beauties of nature, and leaving the imagery of the heathen mythology, of which they are so fond, and which they wield with a richness and facility peculiar to themselves, they give us a touch of the natural, as will be seen in the following, "The Star of Sweet Dundalk;" and observe, Dundalk being a seaport, with a very just and accurate perception of propriety, the poem has been headed with a ship in full sail.

THE STAR OF SWEET DUND-ALK

> In beauteous spring when birds do sing,
> And cheer each mertle shade,
> And shepherds sWains surnades the Planes,
> To find their lambs that stRayed.

This novel application of serenading must strike every one with admiration.

> nigh Roden's Grove I chanced to rove
> To take a rural walk,
>   when to my sight appeared in White
>   the star of sweet dundalk.

The lady having, most luckily for the rhyme, appeared in white, the perambulating lover addresses her; and after having "struggled for to talk" to this most resplendent "Star of Sweet Dundalk," he assures her he is bewildered, and that his heart is bleeding, and thus continues:—

> Your beauteous face my wounds encrase
> And SKin more white than chaLK,
> Makes me regret the day i met
> The STar of sweet dundalk.

But the lady very prudently replies—

> Now sir if I would but cumply
> And give to you my HanD,
> Perhaps that you would prove untrue
> Be pleased to understand

How polite!!—Here she divides our admiration! for we know not whether most to applaud her discretion or her good manners. At length he only requests to become her "slave, poor swain, and friend." This proposition is listened to, but still she is intent on "minding her business, as she ought to do," like the celebrated O'Rafferty, and insists on first "milking her cow;" after which we are favoured with this information:—

> When she had done
> Then off we come
> and carelessly did walk,
> and slowly paced
> To her sweet pLace
> Convaynient to sweet Dundalk.

She then brings him into her father's house, which is "as white as chalk," and (of course) "nigh hand to sweet Dundalk;" and we discover at last, that he has a warm shebeen-house, and a drop of comfort for the traveller, so our hero calls for a glass to drink the health of this "Star of Sweet Dundalk," and enable him, doubtless, to see her charms double; but she still, "minding her business, O'Rafferty-like, hands him a glass; and very dutifully to her father, though, we regret to say, very unsentimentally to her lover, the aforesaid glass

> She mark'd it up in chalk;

and as this must at once destroy all romantic interest in the "Star of Sweet Dundalk," we shall say no more about a heroine that so unworthily degenerates into an avaricious bar-maid. But, by way of counterpoise, we shall give an example of a "holier flame"— and after the money-loving Dundalker, it is really "refreshing" to meet an instance proving the utter devotedness of the female heart, when once imbued with the tender passion. Can there be a more disinterested love than this?

> Oh Thady Brady you are my darlin,
> You are my looking-glass from night till morning,
> I love you better without one fardin
> Than Brian Gallagher wid house and garden.

What fitness, too, there is in the simile, "you are my looking-glass;"—the dearest thing under the sun to a woman.

In the POLEMICAL line, the ballad in Ireland is perfectly national; and no other country, we believe, *sings* polemics; but religion, like love, is nourished by oppression; and hence a cause may be assigned why the Roman Catholic population of Ireland enjoyed, with peculiar zest, the ballads that praised their persecuted faith. But of the many fatal results of the relief bill, not the least deplorable is the "dark oblivion" into which this exalted class of composition is fast passing away. We rejoice to rescue from the corroding fangs of time a specimen in praise of the Virgin Mary, and hitting hard at such ultra Protestants as busied themselves "in the convartin' line," for the good of their brethren:

> The blessed Vergin that we prize
> The fairest fair above the skies
> On her the Heretics tells lies
> When they would make convArsions,

But of the polemical, we candidly confess that we are but ill prepared to speak at large; whether it be that, unlike the gentle Desdemona, we do not "seriously incline," or our early polemico-ballad hunting essays were not successful, we shall not venture to decide. But one evening, at the corner of Mary's-*abbey*—an appropriate place for religious strains—we heard a female ballad-hawker (the men, by-the-bye, do not deal in this line; the Frenchman was right when he said a woman's life was taken up between love and religion)—and whether it was that we could not fairly hear the lady, in consequence of the windows of Ladly's tavern being open, and letting out, along with a stream of very foul air, some very queer air also, that was let out of a fiddle; or that we chanced to fall upon an infelicitous passage in her chant, we cannot say, but the first audible couplet was

> Tran-a-sub-a-stan-a-si-a-ey-a-shin
> Is de fait in which we do Diffind,

and this fairly *bothered* us. Such a jaw-breaker and peace-breaker as transubstantiation—quod versu dicere non est—actually done into verse!!—We took to our heels, and this polysyllabic polemical gave us a distaste for any more controversial cantatas.

In the POLITICAL line, no land abounds in ballads like our own sweet Emerald Isle. In truth, every Irishman is, we verily believe, by birth, a politician. There are many causes assigned for this; and your long-headed philosopher could, no doubt, write a very lengthly article on that head. But it is not our affair at present; suffice it, therefore, to say, politicians they are, and the virus breaks out in divers and sundry ballads, varying in style and subject, according to the strength of the disease in the sufferer. Some abound in laments for Ireland's forlorn condition, but many more are triumphant effusions to the honour and glory of the "men of the people." We remember one *ould* dowager in particular, rather thick in the wind, who wheezed out many a week's work in asthmatic praises of Richard Sheil and Daniel O'Connell, Esquire; but, after the exertion of puffing out one line, she was obliged to pause for breath before giving the following one; and a comical effect was sometimes produced by the lapses, as in the well-known instance of the Scotch precentor. At last when she did come to the burthen of her song, she threatened with a significant shake of her head, which one eye, and a bonnet both black and fiercely cocked, rendered particularly impressive, that

> They (*the parliament*) had better take care about what
>   they are at
> For Shiel is the lad that will give them the chat!
> With a Ballynamona, eroo!—Ballynamona, eroo!
> Ballynamona, eroo!—Brave Shiel and O'Connell for me!

There was a Patagonian fair one of the craft, who patronised Mr O'Counell in particular, always got drunk on the strength of his success, and generally contrived to have a long chorus or burthen to her song, and when, with some difficulty, she picked her way through the difficulties of articulation in each verse, it was very diverting to observe the complacency with which she dropt into the chorus, and seemed to repose herself, as it were, upon its easy monotony, which ran thus:—

> Consill*ar* och hone! och hone! och hone!
> consill*ar* och hone! and och hone-i-o!
> ConSillur och hone! och hone! och hone!
> And its you that can stand alone-i-o!

But the "Shan Van Vogh!" was the grand popular effusion in the great agitator's praise, when he threatened to take the House of Commons by storm at the first election. Of this we may venture to give two verses:—

> Into parliament you'll go, says the Shan Van Vogh,
> To extricate our woe, says the Shan Van Vogh;
> Our foes you will amaze
> And all Europe you will Plaze,
> And owld Ireland's now at *Aise*,
>
> > Says the Shan Van Vogh.

> Our worthy brave O'Connell, says the Shan Van Vogh,
> To have you in we're longing, says the Shan Van Vogh;
> Sure you we well have tried,
> And you're always at our side,
> And you never tuk a bribe,
>
> > Says the Shan Van Vogh.

But the following is one which we cannot resist giving in full, we vouch for its being a true attested copy; and those who do not like to read it, may adopt the practice of the country schoolmaster when he meets a word that proves a jaw-breaker, id est, to "*schkip* and go on."

O'Connell's Farewell Meeting in the Corn-exchange

As O'Connell and Shiels wor convarsin about the rent,
Jack lawless stepp'd in and asked him what news.
Saying are you preparing to go into Parliamint.
Where a loyal Cattolic he can't be refused,
The time is fast approaching when Catholios will take
    their seats;
No Laws can prevant tham Bruns-wiekers are deranged
In the Defince of Britain their loyalty and aid was lent
This conversation passed in the Corn Exchange.

Brave O'Gorman Mahon spoke as the Association did
    begin,
Saying GentlemEn i Pray don't think me rude,
In This month of February how the bigots the will grinn
Like Paul Pry Daniel he drops in you think will he intrud.
The Lawyers of the Minstry they cant prevent his entry,
We know a war with him They'll wage,
In spite of their Dexterity we'll have religious liberty
This converSation passed in the Corn Exchange

Farewell Dearest Danyel Hibernias cOnfidential frind
Our blessin Go along wid you unto the british shore,
Nobility and Gintery to Parliamint will you attind,
Likewise be accompanied with The blessings of the Poor.
Our foes within the house as mute as any mouse,
To see the Agitator Triumphantly arranged,
No ... or factious clan shall daunt the people's man;
This conversation passed in the Corn Exchange.

The worthys, of Hibernia's Ile may fortune On those
    heroes smile,
And every frind in Parliamint That does support the
    claims,

Brave Grattan Plunket and Burdet Brave Anglissy.
We'll never forget this hero's memory in our brest Shall
    ever rEiu.
Here's to maTchless Sheel' and gaʃant Steall, and Noble
    Dawson of Dundalk
The ʃoes oʃ religious liberty thɔ will assail
For the rites oʃ millions The contind, may God protect
    dear Dan onr FrinD.
Pray ʃor his Saʃe return to ould Ireland agin.

These are no contemptible specimens of the political, but they
only bear on our "internal resources," as the parliamentary phrase
is, and evidently were the work of the "secretary for the home
department," in ballad affairs. But be it known unto all men by these
presents, that we have had our "secretary for foreign affairs" also, and
the political chances and changes of Europe have been descanted
upon by the Thomas-street muses of our Balladian Parnassus:
BONAPARTE was the "God of their idolatry," and his victories have
been the theme of their hope and triumph, ingeniously conveyed in
drollery or sarcasm, as his downfall was of their most doleful ditties,
of which we well remember the mournful burthen of one,

> From is throne, och, hoch, hone,
> Like a spalpeen he was hurled.

Yet even in their 'flat despair,' they

> Cast one longing. lingering look behind,

and each verse of another cantata, we have often listened to with
pensive delight, recording his by-gone glories, although it was
wailingly wound up with this dismal though euphonious couplet,

> But he's gone over *saes* and the high mount-i-ayn-ya
> He is gone far away to the Isle of St Helenia.

We hope our readers properly appreciate the fertility of invention and boldness of execution, that produced for the occasion so novel and so able an example of the *callida junctura* of Horace, upon which Bishop Hurd has written so much, as is evinced in this truly musical variety of the common-place word mountain.

Subsequently, however, a strain of jubilee for the re-establishment of Napoleon's dynasty, was long and loudly, though perhaps somewhat prematurely, indulged in; and we well remember hearing the detail of anticipated glories, "many a time and oft," in a certain song, whose exultant chorus, "piercing the night's dull ear," promised great things to the drooping Bonapartists:

When the young King of roome from the court of Vianna
 Will bring his father back from the isle of St Helanna!

As an example of the PATRIOTIC, we picked up a *morçeau* in the "west end," one evening while we stood amongst many admiring and apostrophising auditors, which is quite too rich to give *en masse* to our readers; we would not surfeit them with the good things of the ballad world, and they must be content, therefore, with some extracts from "the bran new ballad," called, by way of title, "The Wild Irishman," which an herculean Hibernian, with a voice like thunder, was pouring from his patriotic throat; he commenced by informing his audience that

When God made the sowl of a wild Irishman
He filled him with love and creations wide span
And gev him perfictions that never is seen
In statue he's matchless—an angel in face.
(*Our friend certainly was an exception.*)
The invy of mankind in iligance and grace
At football and hurlin' agility's sons
(And her daughters so fair, all as spotless as nuns)
When victorious—all mercy—Oh, Erin the green.

Erin the green's forlorn condition was very feelingly depicted in the two succeeding stanzas; and fearing there was no *human* probability of her situation being bettered, the saints were thus characteristically invoked.

> Oh St Patrick, acushla! St Bridget asthore!
> Collum cuil O mavourneen your masther implore,
> To look down with compassion on Erin the green.

This appeal to "*the masther*" is quite irresistible.

But in this it will be perceived there is a mixture of the political mingled with the patriotic; a tint of devotion to party tinged the love of country. The poem having its birth in the *Liberty*, it is possible that the poet, influenced by the localities, wrought his verses as the weaver works his stuff, and so his production is *shot,* as the technical phrase is, with two materials, and reminds us of the alternate flickering of green and red that we see in the national tabinet dresses of our fair countrywomen.

Of the BACCHANALIAN, some falsely imagine "Patrick's Day" to be an example; English people, in particular, suppose "Patrick's Day," in words and music, must be the *beau idéal* of an Irish song—whereas, in neither is it a happy specimen; as for the words, there is amongst them a couplet that pronounces, at once, damning sentence against the whole composition.

> And we will be merry
> And drinking of sherry.

Bah! sherry indeed; no Irish ballad laureat ever wrote two such lines, it is the production of a bungler, especially when we consider that any but a thorough blockhead could have so easily rhymed it thus:—

> And we will be frisky
> A drinking of whiskey
> On Patrick's day in the morning.

"Garryowen," that much superior air, which, in our opinion, ought to be the national one instead, is disfigured, in like manner, by a word which grates harshly upon the ear of the connoisseur:—

> Then come my boys we'll drink brown *ale*
> We'll pay the reck'ning on the nail
> And devil a man shall go to jail
> From Garryowen my glory.

We confess we cannot bear this *ale;* something *ails* us at the sound, and it disturbs our association of ideas; ale, at once, refers us to England; and portly John Bulls and Bonifaces, instead of muscular Paddies, present themselves to our "mind's eye;" it is a pity, for the other lines are good, particularly the third, which displays that noble contempt of the laws so truly characteristic of our heroes of the south. But here follows a touch of the true Bacchanalian, in which our national beverage is victoriously vindicated:—

> The *ould* ladies love coniac
> The sailors all brag of their rum
> It's a folly to talk, Paddy's whack
> Knows there's nothing like whiskey for fun
> They may talk of two birds in a bush,
> But I'd rather have one in the hand,
> For if rum is the pride of the *Sae*
> 'Tis whiskey's the pride of the land.

What a logical deduction is here drawn from a proverb that is "somewhat musty," as our friend Hamlet says—"A bird in the hand is worth two in the bush." Argal, whiskey is much better drinking than rum. The inference is as clear as ditch water.

The bard next proceeds to exult in our superiority over other nations in the native tipple, which he thus felicitously illustrates:—

> The Dutchman he has a big but
> Full of gin, and the munseers drinks port
> To the divil I pitch such rot-gut,
> For to drink it wouldn't be any sport
> 'Tis the juice of the shamrock at home
> That is brew'd in brave Bacchus's still,
> Bates the world, and its of sweet Innishowen
> I wish that I now had my fill.

Here is a happy adaptation of classical knowledge to the subject in hand; Bacchus's *still* is a great hit.

Burns himself indulges in a similar liberty, when he uses his national dialect to name the fount of Castaly:—

> Castalia's *burn*, an' a' that.

But, as the Bacchanalian must be an uninteresting theme to our fair readers, we shall content ourselves with the specimens already given in that line, and hurry on to the next in order of succession, viz. DESCRIPTIVE.

We Irish are fond of dilating on whatsoever subject we treat (perchance, indeed, at this moment we are giving a practical example), and in the descriptive line of ballad, there is "ample verge" for indulging in this natural propensity, whether it concern places or persons, men or manners, town or country, morning, noon, or night. As a specimen in the local line, a brilliant one exists in that far-famed ditty that so pathetically sets forth how

> A Sailor coorted a Farmer's daughter
> That lived Conv*ay*nient to the Isle of Man.

Here, though with that native delicacy which always characterises true genius, the name of the false fair one is withheld, her "local habitation" is considered matter of importance; and with admirable precision it is *laid down*, as seamen say, in the most chart-like fashion,

Convaynient to the Isle of Man.

An additional interest is thus excited for the heroine, who must have been (as far as we could gather from our visit to Douglas, at the late regatta) either a mermaid or some amphibious charmer, whom, with much critical judgment, the poet has selected as the "desaver" of a naval hero.

Another felicitous specimen exists in a very old and favourite ballad, giving "the whole, full, thrue, and partic'lar account" of how a certain highway hero fulfils his *criewel* fate. The description of the entire trial, including the examination of witnesses, is very graphically given; and when sentence of death is at length pronounced against him, you are thus most affectingly informed, in the *first person*:—

> When they did sintence me to Die,
> The Judge and the jury they riz a Murnful cry;
> My Tindher Wife she did roar and Bawl
> While the bitther Tears from her Eyes did fall,
> Oh! the curse o' Jasus light an yez all!

When he comes to the gallows he gives a very exemplary exhortation to "the throng;" and with a sort of a predictive consciousness that he shall live *in verse*, though he must die *in fact*, he addresses to the multitnde, *vivâ voce*, this posthumous appeal:—

> And now *I'm dead*, and let my disgrace
> Be never threw in ny Childher's face,
> For they are Young and desarves no blame
> Altho' their Father is come to shame.

This sudden adoption of the first person is, however, by no means a singular species of metabasis; on the contrary, we find it a favourite figure of speech in such compositions; for example, in "*Thamama Hulla:*"

> I have heerd the town clock give its usual warning
> *I am asleep*, and don't waken me.

And again, in the far-famed "Fanny Blair." The victim of Fanny's false-swearing, after giving this admonitory couplet to all "sportin' young blades"—

> Beware of young women that follys [follows] bad rules
> For that's why I'm cut off in the flower of my bl*u*me,

concludes by very piously ejaculating,

> And now it's your blessin dear parents I crave
> Likewise my dear mother that did me consave.

(He had, it would seem, a supernumerary parent on this occasion)

> And now *I am dead* and laid in the mould
> The Lord may have mercy on my poor sinful So*u*l!

The renowned "Brian O'Lynn" has been the hero of description to a great extent; his apparel even has been deemed worthy of note. Few of our readers, we trust, have had their education so utterly neglected as to be still in ignorance of the first stanza of this incomparable effusion:—

> Brian O'Lynn had no breeches to wear,
> So he bought him a sheepskin to make him a pair;
> With the skinny side out and the woolly side in,
> They are pleasant and cool, says Brian O'Lynn!

But Brian is anxious to cut a figure in the world, and laments the want of that most necessary appendage to "ginteel clothin'"— a watch: but how to come by it is the question. At last Brian hits upon an *expagement* (as a *literary* friend of ours says), which, for originality of invention, leaves rail-roads and steam-carriages far behind. It is with satisfaction that we claim the modest merit of first introducing to public regard and admiration the following inimitable stanza:—

> Brian O'Lynn had no wotch to *put on,*
> So he scooped out a turnip to make him *a one;*
> He next put a cricket cl*a*ne und*h*er the s*h*kin,
> 'Whoo! they'll *think it is tickin',*' says Brian O'Lynn.

Rarissimus Briney! What can surpass this?

But the personal attractions of the fair form the most inexhaustible theme for the poet's fancy, and give a wider scope to his invention in the discovery of apt images: *par exemple*—

> Her waist is taper,
> None is completer
> Like the tuneful nine or the lambs at play;
> And her two eyes shinin
> Like rowlin diamonds,
> And her breath as sweet as the flowers in May.

We cannot too much admire the richness and perspicuity of this description: rich in the display of the lady's charms, which combine the united beauties of the "tuneful nine" with the innocent frolicsomeness of the "lambs at play;" and perspicuous even to the agreeable fact that she has *two eyes*, and both are bright.

But we must not venture to trespass too far on thy patience, gentle reader. On this subject we could never tire of writing, nor shouldst thou of reading, hadst thou but the felicity of being tinctured; like ourselves, with the true ballad passion. But we must

> Lure the tassel-gentle back agin,

and therefore shall hasten to a conclusion for the present.

The NON-DESCRIPT last claims our exemplifying notice, and indeed our memory abounds with illustrations in point; we shall, however, content ourselves with one which we look upon as choice, and deserving to be marked with three R's, as Dominie Sampson says, denoting the rarest excellence:—

THE RHYME FOR THE RAM:

which rhyme is declared to be a mystery far beyond the poet's comprehension, hitherto undiscovered, and to be classed only with the philosopher's stone, or such arcana of nature. We have all heard of the difficulty of finding a rhyme for *silver*, which our countryman overcame at once by adducing *childher* as a satisfactory solution; but the bard on this occasion soars to sublimer flights:

> No one could discover
> From Calais to Dover
> The house of Hanover and the town of Dunleer.
> Nor they who belie us,
> And freedom deny us,
> Ould Mr M——'s could never come near;
> For no Methodist preacher,
> Nor nate linen blacher,
> The keenest of teachers, nor the wisdom of man;
> Nor Joanna Southco*a*t,
> Nor FitzGarild the *pote* [poet]
> Nor *iver* y*i*t wrote a fit rhyme for the Ram.

What a wide range the muse has taken here in search of this rhymatical treasure! In the depths of the sea, between Calais and Dover, she is too straitened: next she throws herself, with as little success, upon the munificence of the house of Brunswick, which, by the most perfect association of ideas in the world, reminds her of the town of Dunleer. The new light is next appealed to unavailingly; and the *wisdom of man* very naturally reminds her of Joanna Southcote, who is surpassed in the climax by that still greater humbug, Fitzgerald the *pote*.

This we fearlessly put forward as the most brilliant specimen of the non-descript in the world.

THE END